SPRING FLOWERS AND APRIL SHOWERS

LITTLE BAMTON BOOK 2

BETH RAIN

Copyright © 2021 by Beth Rain

Spring Flowers and April Showers (Little Bamton Book 2)

First Publication: 18th January, 2021

All rights reserved.

No part of this book may be reproduced in any form or by any electronic or mechanical means, including information storage and retrieval systems. Except for use in any review, the reproduction or utilization of this work, in whole or in part, in any form by any electronic, mechanical or other means now known or hereafter invented, is forbidden without the written permission of the publisher.

Published by Beth Rain. The author may be contacted by email on bethrainauthor@gmail.com

❦ Created with Vellum

CHAPTER 1

'What the hell is that supposed to be?'

Emmy jumped as Marjorie Dawson appeared from the back room of *Daisy Days*, making her fumble with the final knot of the hand-tied bouquet she'd almost finished.

'It's for Andie Jones,' said Emmy, carefully setting the abundance of frothy gypsophila, pink rosebuds, and eucalyptus onto the surface. 'She said she wanted something... a bit different.' The last three words came out in a low mutter. *A bit different* was tantamount to swearing in this time-warp of a shop.

Marjorie was old-school, and not in a good way - no funky vintage retro here! She was firmly stuck in the eighties, where half-dead carnations ruled and customers had to choose which arrangement they wanted from the dozen or so styles they offered in their laminated catalogue.

'She wanted something *different?*' hissed Marjorie, her iron-grey curls quivering.

Emmy nodded, letting out a quiet little sigh. Déjà vu. They'd had this argument too many times to count over the past three years.

'Tell me, you useless lump, did you even show her the catalogue?'

Emmy shrugged. Marjorie had a knack for turning her twenty-nine-year-old professional self into a stroppy teen. It was either that or have a damn good cry, and Emmy didn't think she had any tears left in her after the week she'd just had.

'Don't just shrug at me!' said Marjorie, her coral-pink lips coming together in a disapproving cat's-bum. 'You know if someone wants something *different,* we offer them The Duchess!'

Emmy bit down on her lip to stop herself from saying something she'd regret. The Duchess was their most expensive monstrosity. Pink and white carnations placed into a heart-shaped basket, finished off with gypsophila, more ribbon than you could shake a stick at, and a pair of bright-pink plastic birds. It was truly hideous, and Emmy held it as a matter of personal pride that, in all the time she'd put up with Marjorie, she'd never once recommended The Duchess.

'Well?' Marjorie demanded.

Emmy cleared her throat. 'Andie wanted something… a bit lighter? More modern?'

Marjorie sniffed and snatched up the beautiful

bouquet from the counter. She turned it slowly, looking like she was about to throw up.

'Well, these are wasted. I'll take the cost out of your next paycheque. Let me make this clear for one last time - *you* work for *me.* You are untrained, unskilled, and you're very lucky to have a job here given what I have to put up with. No other florist would touch you with a barge pole. This is the last time, Emmeline. You know that we only work from the catalogue! If I catch you wasting stock on something like *this* again,' she shoved the bunch of flowers close to Emmy's face, 'I will be forced to let you go.' Marjorie turned and lobbed them into the bin behind the counter.

There was complete silence in the little shop for a moment. Emmy couldn't take her eyes off the bin where she could see tiny white flowers and a few blue-grey leaves just peeping out over the top. After everything that had already happened to her this week, this was the last straw. She'd had enough. Life was too short to put up with this kind of shit. But no - she couldn't think like that. She needed this job - now more than ever.

The jangle of the bell behind her alerted Emmy to a new customer, and she quickly tried to plaster some kind of welcoming smile onto her face.

'What are you doing, just standing there?' hissed Marjorie. 'See to your customer! Can't I even trust you with the basics anymore? I'll go and put together a Duchess basket for Andie's order.'

Marjorie disappeared into the back room and Emmy drew in a long, slow breath. This job should fill her full of hope and romance and joy. Instead, it had turned her into a worn-down cynic. The flowers themselves didn't help. Emmy adored flowers and had done ever since she'd helped her Grandad Jim tend his wonderful walled garden when she was little. But the flowers here were nothing like the fragrant blooms they'd used to pick by the armful for her Nan - who would blush and beam and bury her nose in them every single time.

The flowers they sold in the shop arrived in a giant lorry. Like most commercial flowers they were picked abroad and dunked in goodness knows how many chemicals - from fungicide to silver nitrate - all so that they could be shipped and stored and last as long as possible. In her heart, Emmy longed to work with local, seasonal flowers - full of colour and scent and life. Sadly, that just wasn't how things were done.

She eyeballed the newcomer who was hovering near the individual flower buckets and sized him up. This one was an easy guess: guilty cheat.

It was a game Emmy had been playing ever since she'd started at *Daisy Days*. Most customers fell into specific categories - the men especially. Last-minute gift; heartfelt apology; family flowers; guilty cheat; flowers for the mistress; devoted husband. The last category was her favourite to serve, but sadly they had been few and far between recently.

There had been a time when she'd enjoyed guessing what a customer was looking for - but now it just made her feel sad and tired. She knew that this particular customer would look at everything from the deep red roses to the expensive lilies, only to settle for one of their cheap and not-so-cheerful pre-made bunches to present to his long-suffering wife. She would go so far as to guess that he'd be back in for roses and lilies within the next fortnight. Flowers for the mistress.

She sighed and stepped forward.

'Can I help you?' she asked, polite-mode activated.

He swept his eyes down the full length of her, then rested his gaze on her chest. Eew!

'I'm looking for something nice. Something for my wife,' he said with a lazy smile.

Emmy shuddered slightly. 'Roses,' she said, knowing full well he wouldn't go for it. 'You can never go wrong with a dozen roses - maybe mix reds and pinks?'

He raised his eyebrows. 'How much would that cost?'

Emmy gave him the price and he quickly shook his head. 'Nah - how about one of the bunches from outside the door?'

Bingo. She was right again. 'Sure,' she said.

'Great. I'll take them now, but do you do deliveries too?'

Emmy nodded.

'Wonderful. Can I get three dozen red roses delivered tomorrow?'

Emmy nodded again. Maybe she *had* been wrong. 'Of course,' she said. 'I can take the payment and delivery details from you now.'

The guy followed her over to the counter.

'Can I take your name and number?'

'Is that necessary?' he said, looking surprised.

Emmy frowned and nodded. 'Just in case there's a problem with the delivery.'

'Oh, okay. It's Alec Davies, and I'll give you my mobile number.'

'Lovely. And if I can take Mrs Davies' first name - for the delivery?'

'Er,' he shuffled, 'the, erm, the delivery is for a friend of ours.'

Emmy looked up from the order form and stared at him. The guy stared back at her, then smirked and gave a little shrug. 'You know how it is.'

Emmy put her pen down. 'Yes. I do. Unfortunately, Mr Davies, I've just remembered that we won't be getting enough roses in tomorrow's shipment to fulfil your order.'

'Excuse me?!' he spluttered in confusion.

'We won't be able to do your delivery for you,' she said slowly and deliberately.

'But you've got enough in here now-'

'I'm sure you don't want your *friend* to receive old flowers?' she said, keeping her face as straight as she could.

'I... I...'

'But you can still get your wife something beautiful today. *That's* the most important thing really, isn't it?' she said with exaggerated innocence.

'Forget it! I'll go somewhere else,' he huffed.

'Have a nice day!' said Emmy in a ringing tone, sneering at his back as he strode out of the shop.

'Emmeline!'

Oh, crap.

'What did you just do?!'

Emmy swallowed and turned to face her boss.

'I...'

'No - I don't want to hear it.'

Emmy crossed her arms defensively. 'He's cheating on his wife.'

'That's none of your business!' snapped Marjorie. 'You just cost me a large order. I've had enough. This is the last time-'

'You're right, it is,' Emmy interrupted. Her voice was quiet but steady with the certainty that she couldn't stand to be in this place a moment longer than she had to be. She stepped forward and scooped the bunch of flowers back out of the rubbish bin, gently stroking a couple of bent stems back into place as best as she could. She cradled them in the crook of her arm like an injured pet.

'What do you think you're doing?' Marjorie squeaked.

'Taking my flowers home,' she said in the same flat tone. She stepped around Marjorie, walked through to the back room and gathered her coat and handbag with her free arm.

'You're not due a break!' Marjorie's face appeared at the door looking like a confused strawberry.

'Yes. Yes, I am. I need a break from this place. From you. From all this sh…' Emmy stopped herself. 'I'm done, Marjorie. I'm leaving.'

'Don't be ridiculous - we have a wedding at the weekend!'

Emmy stared at her boss of three years, trying to muster some kind of sympathy for dropping her in it - and completely failed.

'Marjorie, you just said that you'd had enough. I have too. Anyway I'm sure you and Alice will manage perfectly well without me on Saturday,' she said, trying to contain a smirk at the idea of Marjorie and her octogenarian Saturday "girl" managing an entire wedding without her. 'After all - I am just an "untrained, useless lump."'

'I… I…' spluttered Marjorie. 'You can't just *go*! You need to give me notice, or I won't pay you!'

'Okay. I understand,' said Emmy.

'Good.' Marjorie nodded in relief, clearly thinking she'd won the argument.

'You take care, Marjorie.' Emmy pulled her bag more firmly onto her shoulder, adjusted the flowers in her arms and walked calmly past her old boss and across the shop floor with its faded displays. The sound of the bell ringing behind her as she closed the door added an almost comedic finality to the proceedings.

As Emmy strode down the dishevelled, partially-abandoned high street, she broke into a huge smile. She was finally free.

CHAPTER 2

Sadly, the smile didn't last for very long. The initial relief at having escaped Marjorie's clutches had already started to wear off by the time she let herself into her little second-floor flat. The reality of what she'd done was starting to crash down on her.

She paused in her hallway, kicked off her shoes and dumped her handbag before padding through to the kitchenette to find a vase for her flowers. She pulled a vintage enamelled jug out from the cupboard under the sink, filled it with water and arranged them - carefully removing the few sprigs that had been damaged by their unwelcome trip into the dustbin. She popped these shorter lengths into a glass vase on the windowsill. They deserved to be enjoyed as much as the rest - it wasn't their fault that Marjorie had no taste and even less tact.

Marjorie. A thorn in her side that was finally gone.

She could still feel the initial flood of joy - but it was already being buried under a landslide of practicalities.

Emmy let out a huge sigh and made herself a cup of tea. It was time to take stock.

She carried her mug through to the tiny living room and curled up on her corner of the sofa - though technically, as of a week ago, the whole sofa was her domain. Ever since Chris had stood up that Thursday night, announced that he was off out, and had never come back.

At the time, Emmy had just assumed that he'd headed down to the pub to meet his mates. Things had been strained between them for several months, so the fact that he hadn't told her where he was going didn't really register. She had settled down uncomfortably to watch a film and await his return and the inevitable argument that would follow. Only - it didn't.

At 10.30pm, just as she was considering disappearing off to bed, a text had pinged onto her phone.

In case you haven't figured it out, we're over. I've moved in with Julie. Will arrange to collect remaining stuff.

And that had been that. A five-year relationship ended in the space of twenty words. She didn't really know how she felt about it yet. Every time her brain went to prod the open wound, she closed down and retreated into practical mode. Like - how was she supposed to pay the rent without his contribution. And the bills? And… everything.

Now, without her job, at least the answer had

become a simple one. She could no longer afford to live here.

She stared around at the living room and a wave of sadness washed over her. She'd spent so much time in here with Chris, planning their future. Now, all that was left of their life together were the books and DVDs that surrounded her, balanced on every available surface. She'd been separating his stuff from hers, but she'd given up halfway through, leaving the place littered with teetering piles.

Emmy uncurled her legs, leant forward, carefully placed her mug down on the table in front of her and burst into tears.

She wrapped her arms around herself and rocked quietly as the sobs overtook her. She wasn't really sure what she was crying about. Chris leaving? Losing her job? Being forced to make decisions she didn't feel grown-up enough to make? All of the above.

She took several deep breaths until her breathing began to calm down, even if her tears weren't showing any signs of letting up. She'd never been much of a crier before, but over the past week, it was like she'd sprung a leak.

She got up, went to the kitchen for a handful of kitchen roll to mop her face. She grabbed her mobile from the counter while she was at it and headed back to the sofa. She needed to talk to her mum.

'Bollocks!' she sobbed as her leg brushed against one of the piles of books on the coffee table and they tumbled onto her feet. She squatted down to gather them back up, but the sight of the one on the top of the heap made her pause. It was a book about growing cut flowers. It had landed splayed open at the title page, and there in front of her, in Grandad Jim's best, loopy handwriting, was a message he'd written for her on her eighth birthday.

Follow your dreams, Emmy-Lou
Then your life will always be full of flowers.
Happy birthday,
Love Grandad Jim

Emmy gently picked it up and stroked the message with the tip of her finger. She missed him so much - her lovely Grandad Jim who had known her better than anyone else in the world. She felt like she'd let him down. He'd always encouraged her to be herself, no matter what - and no matter how much she was trying to ignore the fact, she had to admit to herself that she'd been doing the exact opposite for several years. Pretending to be someone she wasn't.

She carefully laid the book back down onto the coffee table and rushed through to her bedroom. Ignoring the black bags at the end of the bed where she'd dumped Chris's clothes the previous evening, Emmy rummaged in her bottom drawer and pulled out the thick Aran jumper that had once belonged to Grandad Jim. She peered at herself in the full-length mirror for a moment and pulled a face before tugging off the prissy little dress that was so *not* her, it was funny. She tugged on an old pair of jeans, comfy tee-shirt and topped it off with the jumper.

She smoothed her long, red hair back out of her face and let out a sigh of relief. That was more like it! If this week had taught her anything, it was that she needed to remember who she really was. Emmy-Lou - complete with scruffy jumpers, bobble hats and, if she could manage it, earth beneath her feet and under her fingernails! She had a plan. It was time to call her mum.

'Hello, lovely girl!' Her mum's customary greeting felt like an instant hug. She sounded like she was sitting right next to her rather than oceans away, living the life of Riley with her lover in Portugal. 'How are you doing, Emmy love? Unusual time of day for you to be calling...'

The woman didn't miss a trick.

'I walked out on Marjorie,' said Emmy, her voice wobbling slightly.

'Good for you love!' her mum said warmly. 'About time you left that awful shop! Well, what did that battle-axe do to finally push you over the edge?'

'The usual - she binned a bouquet I'd just finished. It wasn't that though - I think I was just at the end of my tether after everything, you know?!'

'I know love,' her mum said gently. And she did know. Because just a week ago, Emmy had been wailing at her down the phone about Chris leaving. Her mum had been incredibly kind, but a lot less surprised than Emmy had expected.

'You know Chris and I were saving up to buy a house together? That's why I stuck with the stupid job for so long. Chris reckoned it was better for me to have something steady rather than-'

'Doing what you actually wanted to do?'

Emmy nodded, forgetting for a moment that her mum couldn't actually see her.

'Look,' said her mum, 'I know that you probably don't want to hear this yet Em - but that boy was bad for you. You've not been yourself for far too long - ever since he turned up, in fact.'

Emmy opened her mouth to agree but her mum got there first.

'I was talking to your Aunty Ali about this just yesterday. We both said that you need a change. I know it probably doesn't feel like it right now, but maybe this has all been for the best.'

'Actually, I agree,' said Emmy, finally managing to squeeze a word in edgeways as her mum stopped to draw breath.

'You do?!' said her mum in surprise.

'Yes,' said Emmy. 'Anyway, what's happened today answers one of the questions I've been struggling with since Chris left. I definitely can't afford this place now.'

'What are you going to do, love?' Asked her mum quietly.

'Actually, I just got a bit of a wake-up call from Grandad Jim.'

'From dad?! Emmy, I don't-'

'Don't panic, I haven't lost the plot,' Emmy chuckled at the concern in her mum's voice. 'I just found a message he wrote to me in an old gardening book.'

'Oh, right - lovely!' said her mum, relief evident in her voice. 'So what did it say?'

'To follow my dreams,' said Emmy simply. She brought the cuff of Grandad Jim's jumper up to her face and rested her cheek against it for a moment, fighting back the tingle of tears. 'I really miss him, mum.'

'Oh love. He thought the world of you, you know?'

'I know,' said Emmy with a little sob as a stray tear escaped and made its way onto the jumper. She cleared her throat. 'I've got an idea. A bit of a plan.'

'Ooh, that sounds promising! Care to share?'

'Well, is Aunty Ali still off to stay with her friend in Australia soon?'

'Yes - next week!' said her mum.

'Has she managed to find anyone to look after Dragonfly Cottage yet?' Nerves suddenly swooped in Emmy's stomach. This plan had to work. She needed to go back to Little Bamton. That was where she remembered being happiest. Where she'd truly been herself.

What better way to recapture that than to stay for a while in Dragonfly Cottage?

It was where her mum and Aunty Ali had grown up. Dragonfly had belonged to her grandparents, and it had been like a second home to her when she was little too. She'd loved nothing more than working alongside her Grandad in the walled garden at the back of the cottage, sharing cups of tea with him in his potting shed. The place belonged to Aunty Ali now, but her Aunt had always made sure that she knew how welcome she was, anytime she fancied a visit. Emmy felt a wave of guilt wash over her. She hadn't been back since Grandad Jim had died.

'I know it's really last minute and she's bound to have sorted something out by now - but you mentioned about a month ago that Aunty Ali was struggling to find someone to look after Charlie while she's gone.'

'She's not found anyone to actually stay there, but she's got a chap who's going to be doing some work on the cottage while she's away, and he's offered to feed Charlie. I think she'd be much happier if there was someone there to keep him company though. Is that what you were thinking, Em?'

'Well... yes!' Said Emmy, working hard not to jump up and down in excitement. Three months in beautiful Devon looking after Ali's fat, pampered cat? It sounded a bit like heaven compared to this flat full of bad memories and exorbitant bills. 'Do you know how much rent Aunty Ali would be looking for?' she asked.

'Rent? Don't be silly Emmy! You'd be doing her a favour as much as she would be doing you one. And anyway, you're family and family stick together. Do you want me to call her with the good news?'

Emmy couldn't help it - she burst into tears again, but this time, they were happy ones. It took her several seconds to calm down enough to finally answer her mother. 'Yes. Yes please.'

CHAPTER 3

The journey down to Devon was a complete blur. Emmy was already knackered after a week of intensive packing, charity shop runs, and scrubbing the Bristol flat so that she could hand over the keys. She'd finished at last, and rather than being sad to leave, it was actually a huge weight off her mind.

The place had still been half-full of Chris's stuff when she'd left, but frankly, she couldn't give a rat's arse what the estate agent and landlord decided to do with it all. He'd paid the deposit, so if he was too lazy to sort himself out, that was his lookout.

Emmy had very quickly discovered that cramming all her worldly goods into her tiny, clapped out old car made for an extremely uncomfortable trip down the dual carriageway. She was cramped, hemmed in and sitting at a very weird angle, as she'd had to move the driving seat forward just so that she could fit everything in.

She'd parted company with as many things as she could face giving to the charity shop around the corner - as well as a couple more further afield when the first one said it had run out of space for any more donations. Still, all the bits and pieces she'd kept had added up. The car was packed all way up to the roof.

By the time Emmy took the turning into Little Bamton, she could swear that the crick in her neck had become a permanent fixture. She was longing for a long, hot soak in the bath and maybe a celebratory glass of wine or two.

As she reached the junction at the funny, double-hump-backed bridge, she thought back to the long hours she'd spent as a kid, fishing over the side with a rod Grandad Jim had made for her from a bean pole, a length of garden twine and a bent pin. Of course, she hadn't caught a single thing, but she'd loved sitting there, side-by-side with him, watching the water trickle beneath them. Emmy smiled softly and turned left onto the narrow lane that led up to Dragonfly Cottage.

She pulled off into the gravel parking-spot and breathed a huge sigh of relief as she killed the engine. The resulting silence was bliss, and Emmy rested her head back for a couple of seconds, just staring through the windscreen at the familiar, friendly thatched cottage. Just the sight of the little porch around the front door was like a balm to her jangled nerves. She knew that come June, it would be smothered in sweet-smelling, blowsy pink roses.

Emmy grabbed her handbag, threw open the car door and stepped out with some difficulty, her legs having cramped up on the drive. She stretched her arms above her head, staring all the while at the pretty front garden which seemed to be glowing with its profusion of daffodils.

This was her idea of heaven. Sure, her life may have fallen apart spectacularly, but right now, in this moment, she felt a bubble of happiness rise up in her chest. She was home. Really and truly home.

Emmy decided to leave everything in the car and make herself a cuppa before facing the mammoth task of finding somewhere to stash all her belongings in the cottage.

She made her way up the garden path and ran her fingers along a high, dusty ledge in the porch. The spare cottage key had been kept there for as long as she could remember. Rather trusting of her aunt, Emmy thought, to continue the tradition, but then how many people drove down this quiet lane in a day? She groped around until her fingers closed around the key, waiting for her just as her aunt had promised.

She fitted it into the lock, pushed the door open - and jumped. Charlie, her aunt's huge black and white cat, was sitting in the hallway, staring at her with an accusatory, owlish look on his face.

'Hey Charlie!' she crooned, her voice feeling strangely loud as it echoed off the flagstone floor. The cat simply stared at her and swiped his tail a couple of times.

Ah. Wasn't Charlie meant to be a friendly cat? Wasn't that the whole point of this? Cosy cottage, friendly moggy, a chance to rediscover who she was?

Emmy's daydream of curling up in an armchair with Charlie on her lap quickly disappeared. She took a cautious step forward and the cat stood up, turned his back on her, gave a half-hearted hiss of contempt over his shoulder and sauntered off up the stairs. Bloody charming.

She shrugged. Ah well. She would feed him, keep him alive and maybe forget about trying to make friends. She was the interloper here after all. She'd simply have to play cat-slave and not expect any snuggles in return.

Emmy peeped around the doorway to her left. The living room had barely changed since she was a kid. The slates of the hallway gave way to warm, wooden floorboards covered in brightly striped rag-rugs. There were two, giant squashy sofas that had always been more about comfort than style, and together with the granny-squared crochet blankets that were still in evidence, they'd made some spectacular forts when she was a little girl.

The open fireplace she'd been absolutely obsessed with now played host to a gorgeous wood burner - and

Emmy could already imagine snuggling down under a blanket with a fire glowing behind those little windows. But not right now. Now she needed to wash the dust of the journey off and treat herself to a much-needed cup of tea. She headed back out into the hallway and through to the large kitchen on the other side.

Again, it looked no different to when her grandparents had been alive. The large, scrubbed-pine table still stood right in the middle of the room, and there was a beautiful old butler's sink set beneath the back window. Emmy wandered over and peered out. Well, if you had to wash up, that was definitely the view to do it to.

The window overlooked her Grandad Jim's pride and joy - a large walled garden. It had been glorious when he'd been alive, and as she gazed out at it, Emmy was greeted with the sight of beautifully pruned rose bushes with fresh spring leaves, bare-limbed fanned fruit trees trained against the walls and more daffodils than you could shake a stick at. Clearly, Ali lavished just as much love on it as Grandad Jim had.

Towards the back of the garden, she could just make out the shape of the stone potting shed. That had been Grandad Jim's favourite haunt, and she'd spent many hours with him out there, helping him to sow seeds and pot up seedlings. There had been a little gas Primus and an old kettle, and there had been nothing more delicious than a tin mug full of tea, sitting side by side on the old wooden stools with her grandad, his tinny old radio on low in the background. There was a huge part of her that wanted to rush right out there and surround herself in childhood memories. But what if it had changed? She wasn't sure she would be able to deal with that today. She would save that particular visit for another time.

Emmy sucked in a deep breath and fought the sudden prickle of tears. So far, this had been a truly shitty year, but now that she was here it felt like something, somehow, might be going right at long last.

Remembering her mission, she quickly filled the electric kettle from the tap, popped it onto the base and flicked it on. Deciding she may as well go and take a peep at her bedroom while she was waiting for it to boil, she headed back out into the hallway and made her way up the stairs, trailing her fingers along the warm, glossy wood of the age-polished bannister.

Dragonfly Cottage had two bedrooms - well, two and a half if you counted the little box room that had been hers as a kid. It had had a funny, raised bed with a built-in writing desk underneath in. There had been something magical about climbing up the wooden ladder to bed. Grandad Jim had helped her stick glow-in-the-dark stars to the ceiling, and they'd always made her feel so warm and cosy as she'd drifted off to sleep. She wondered if they were still there.

Aunty Ali had suggested that Emmy take the spare room at the front of the house. Ali had eventually moved into the master bedroom at the back of the cottage after Grandad Jim had passed away, as she loved being able to look out over the walled garden while enjoying a cup of tea in bed.

Emmy didn't mind where she slept - just the fact that she was back in this beautiful cottage, filled with happy memories, was a balm compared to the flat in Bristol. She'd realised, as she'd been moving her things out, that she'd come to hate the place. It just reminded her how fast things between her and Chris had deteriorated.

Emmy gave herself a little shake. She didn't want to think about all that now. Today was about brand new starts, and Chris had no place here.

She hurried along the hallway to her room and pushed open the door. It was light, bright and fresh, with its white walls, simple forget-me-not curtains and matching bed-linen. There was a vintage Lloyd Loom chair over in the corner next to a sturdy, pine chest of drawers.

Emmy went over to the windows and stared out at the front garden. Across the lane and she could just see over the hedge into the paddock that belonged to Dragonfly Cottage. Her aunt had said she could use it for anything she fancied while she was there. She'd even suggested camping, which had made Emmy laugh as she'd spent many hours begging to pitch a tent over there when she was little. Now, with the comforts of the cottage surrounding her, the idea of sleeping under canvas was a lot less tempting than it had been all those years ago.

This room would suit her down to the ground, and there was plenty of space to stack all her bags and boxes up against the wall for now, until she found somewhere more permanent to live. She sighed. She'd only just got here and she was already worrying about what she'd do when she had to leave. She hastily put the thought out of her head. She was determined to make the most of every second she had here at Dragonfly Cottage.

As she turned away from the windows, her foot caught on something and she stumbled. Huh. There was a beaten-up old duffel bag resting on the stripped floorboards that she hadn't spotted. Perhaps Ali had popped it in here when she was packing for her trip and forgotten about it. Emmy bent down and lifted it carefully. Crikey, it weighed a ton! She heaved it over to the chair and lifted it up out of the way. She'd check it out later - after she'd had that cuppa.

Back out in the hallway, Emmy headed towards the bathroom at the end of the hall and pushed the door.

'Shit!' she squeaked as it flew open and crashed into the airing cupboard doors behind it.

'Fuck!' a matching grunt came from the other side of the bathroom, as a tousled, dark head shot up in surprise and promptly bashed into the underside of the hand-basin with a resounding crack.

CHAPTER 4

There on the floor, rubbing his head while muttering a string of obscenities, was a man. A very surprised, very pissed-off looking man.

'Who're you!' demanded Emmy, her voice sharp with the shock of finding out that she wasn't alone in the cottage.

'You must be Emmy?' he muttered, getting to his feet, still rubbing his head.

She nodded, confused.

'I'm Jon. Ali said you'd be arriving sometime today so I wanted to finish getting this new basin plumbed in before you needed it. Sorry - didn't think you'd be here until later.'

'Oh. Right.' Jon? *This* was the plumber her aunt had said would be working on the cottage?! Oh dear. Oh dear, dear, dear. She was in big trouble. He wasn't meant to look like *this* - like Aiden Turner crossed with a pirate crossed with... with... nope, she couldn't put her finger on it. He was simply the most beautiful man she'd ever laid eyes on. Oh crap, this wasn't meant to happen.

Emmy realised that she was staring and cleared her throat awkwardly. 'Are you okay?' she asked as she watched him run his fingers through his hair, clearly feeling for any signs of blood or a bump.

'I'm fine,' he said with a grin, dropping his hand. 'I just wasn't expecting a banshee at the door!'

'And I wasn't expecting... well... you!'

'You weren't?' His grin dropped and he looked worried. 'I thought Ali might have mentioned...'

'Oh, she mentioned that you'd be doing some work while I stayed here - I just didn't realise that you... that you...' what was she going to say? *That you'd be so bloody gorgeous?* 'That you'd have a key,' she finished lamely.

'Of course I do!' he laughed. 'How else would I get in?'

Emmy shook her head. She needed to re-group and fast. 'Look, I'm in dire need of a cup of tea. Fancy one?'

Jon raised his eyebrows. 'Er... sure, okay. I'll be down in just a couple of minutes when I've finished off here,' he said, pointing vaguely at the basin. 'Oh - did you need to use the bathroom?'

Emmy shook her head and, feeling a quick, hot blush paint her cheeks, turned on her heel and headed back down to the kitchen as fast as she could.

Huh, so her little oasis wasn't going to be quite as

calm and peaceful as she'd hoped, not if Jon had his own key and was going to be able to come and go as he pleased. How was she supposed to kick back, relax and slob around when a gorgeous man might appear at any moment?

Aunty Ali had explained that he'd be around quite a bit in order to get the new central heating installed, but she'd not expected him to have free run of the place. Never mind, it wasn't a big deal. Ali might not have set any boundaries but she could have a chat with Jon about it herself. She just needed to keep her head screwed on and not let that ridiculously chiselled chin and dark crop of hair throw her off her game.

She flicked the kettle back on, grabbed two cups and slammed them down onto the worktop rather harder than she meant to. She was angry with herself. She'd completely sworn off men after the horror that had been the past few months. She didn't want their friendship, she didn't want them in her space, and she definitely didn't want another relationship. Yet here she was, less than an hour into her lovely three-month extended holiday, and there was already a man on the scene making her tingle!

Emmy hunted around for the teabags and then sighed, wishing she'd thought to bring a bottle of milk and a few basics with her. She opened the fridge without much hope, and to her surprise spotted a fresh bottle of milk, some cheese, ham and a range of veggies in the bottom drawer. Surely her aunt hadn't had the time to go shopping before she'd headed off on her great adventure?

'Finding your way around okay?'

Jon's voice at the door made her jump again. Second time in ten minutes.

'Yeah. Fine thanks. Not much has changed since I stayed here as a kid,' she said, turning to him and forcing a smile.

He grinned back, then he bent down to scoop up a purring Charlie, who'd been winding his way in and out of Jon's legs, rubbing his face all over him.

'Huh,' grunted Emmy, 'looks like you've got a fan!'

'Me and old Charlie have come to an arrangement,' he said with a grin, scruffing the old cat's head, much to the fluffy traitor's obvious delight.

'Which is?'

'I give him treats and plenty of cuddles … and he lets me,' laughed Jon.

Emmy turned her back on the pair of them and added milk to the two cups of tea, pausing when she realised she hadn't even asked him if he took milk.

She turned back to him, bottle still in hand with the question on her face.

Jon nodded. 'And two sugars please.'

'Oh … erm…' she said, unsure if there was any.

'I left a new pack in the cupboard just there,' he pointed above her head. 'I did a bit of shopping for you, just so you had some basics.'

'Oh!' Emmy turned back to him in surprise. 'Thanks, that's really kind of you.'

Jon shrugged. 'It's no bother. Didn't think you'd fancy driving to the nearest town just so you could have a cuppa and some breakfast in the morning. There's fresh eggs, bread, butter, a couple of tins and some dried stuff in the cupboard too.'

'What do I owe you?' she said, popping his cup of tea down near him and going to reach for her handbag, hoping that she still had a bit of cash in there.

Jon shook his head. 'Don't worry about that! If you don't mind me using it too when I stop for lunch, and you get the next lot in, then we're sorted.'

'Oh, sure. Okay.' Emmy's heart sank. This was feeling less and less like her cosy hideaway in the country and more like some weird house-share. She wasn't sure she was up for that. Then a thought dawned on her.

'Jon - are you living in the house too? Ali didn't say…'

Jon shook his head but Emmy thought she saw a shadow cross his face. 'No, she did offer originally but then you needed a place, so I stayed put.'

Emmy's heart sank. 'Oh no. I'm so sorry, I didn't…'

'Don't apologise!' he said, picking up his mug and taking a grateful swig of tea. 'It's no big deal. You're her niece - you come first,' he shrugged. 'Of course you do.'

'But - what about you?'

'I've got my caravan in the paddock over the lane.

That's why I'm doing the work for Ali - part of our agreement.'

'Oh, okay.' Hm. Maybe it wasn't just Charlie who saw her as an unwelcome guest.

'It's fine, really,' he said, catching the uncertain look on her face. 'It wouldn't really have made sense for me to get comfy for a couple of months only to have to move out again when Ali comes back. It works for you because you're just visiting, but Little Bamton is my home, so if I'm going to move out of the caravan, I need to find something a bit more permanent I guess.' He stopped for a moment to take a sip of tea. 'Anyway, it's all good. It's spring now, and the weather's already starting to warm up a bit. As long as you don't mind me making use of the washing machine and the shower, then we're fine.'

What?!

It wasn't that she minded sharing the facilities, but he'd be... naked... and... and...

Pull yourself together, Emmy!

She was an adult. She could totally handle the idea of a naked man showering in the same house as her. Of course she could. Of *course* she could! Anyway, it didn't look like she was going to get much choice in the matter, did it?!

'Of course,' she finally choked out, her face flaming as the image of him, naked in the shower, lodged itself firmly in her mind's eye.

'You okay?' he asked, a look of concern crossing his face. 'You look a bit ... peculiar.'

Charming!

'Maybe you should sit down for a moment - you've had a bit of a drive, haven't you?' he asked.

'Bristol,' she said shortly, burying her nose in her tea and trying to get the soapy image of him out of her head.

Jon nodded. 'Far enough. So ... are we expecting your other half as well? Ali didn't say...'

Emmy flinched. On one hand, she guessed she should be grateful that her Aunt hadn't shared her private life with the whole village, but on the other hand, it meant that she had to actually talk about it to complete random strangers.

'No. No other half,' she said, catching Jon's eye.

'Oh! Sorry ... I just assumed ...' Jon looked a bit thrown for some reason.

Emmy shrugged. 'There was. Now there isn't. Part of the reason I'm here.' There, that was plenty of information. He knew that some random bloke wasn't about to turn up at the cottage, and that was as much as he needed to know. 'Look, I'd better get my stuff in from the car,' she said.

'Did you bring much?' he asked, striding over and popping his cup on the draining board.

Emmy let out an involuntary laugh. 'Only everything I own.'

'Oh, crikey!'

'Yep - I had to give back the keys to my flat before I left. I didn't want to pay for storage so anything that I couldn't bear to give away, I crammed into the back of the car. I think I've stocked the charity shops near my old place for at least a decade!'

'I can give you a hand to bring everything in if you'd like?' Jon offered.

'Erm…' Emmy's mind instantly flew to the dozens of *Bags For Life* in the back of the car, holding everything from her bathroom products to the contents of her underwear drawer. She *really* didn't want him getting a glimpse into those - for his sanity as well as hers! 'Thanks … I might take you up on that when I get down to the heavier bits later. But I'll deal with the smaller bits first.'

'Oh, okay, no probs,' he said lightly.

Great, now she'd managed to offend him. Emmy gave a little, mental sigh. She'd been expecting an easy, man-free three months where she didn't have to worry about denting fragile egos.

'I'm really grateful,' she said quickly, 'it's just - I kinda bundled everything into the car at the end, so there's random stuff just wrapped in jumpers and towels wedged in all over the place.'

Jon chuckled. 'Fair enough. It sounds like you know the method behind your madness. Just give me a shout if you need an extra pair of hands, okay? Oh - and don't trip over my bag - I left it in the spare room.'

'I wondered about that - I moved it onto the chair earlier. I thought Ali might have left it in there.'

Jon shook his head. 'Nah, it's just some bits and pieces I needed to finish off the bathroom today and my shower stuff.'

'Right.' And there he was again, naked and soapy in her brain. What was wrong with her?!

'Are you sure you're okay? Why don't you leave unpacking until later and have a nap or something?'

Emmy shook her head. 'I'm fine. The fresh air will do me good!'

CHAPTER 5

By the time Emmy had made what felt like her thousandth trip from the car to her new bedroom, she wished that she'd been even more strict with herself when it came to getting rid of stuff. What had started out as a lovely, airy, bright room now felt cluttered and full of junk.

She stopped for a moment and mopped her sweaty face with her sleeve, staring at the mound of bags and boxes. It felt a bit like her old life, the one she was desperately trying to leave behind in Bristol, had followed her here. She made an executive decision… when it came to unpacking, she would only keep out the things that she really needed or wanted to have around her. All the rest could go back in the boxes. But that was a job for later.

She'd finished bringing up most of the stuff from

the car. There were just the heavier bits of furniture and books left to shift inside now... and they could wait for later on. She needed a break.

She scooted out into the hallway, closing her bedroom door behind her. It wasn't that she didn't trust Jon - but no one needed to see the chaotic mess she was in right now!

'Jon?' she called softly at the bathroom door, determined not to make him jump again and add another injury to his list.

'Need a hand?' he called back.

There was a scuffling sound the other side, then he pulled the door open. Charlie glared up at her from the bath mat. Clearly he'd decided to play plumber's mate for the day.

'I'm good for now thanks. I've only got a couple of bits left to bring in, but I need a break so they can stay there until later - or maybe even tomorrow. I just wanted to let you know I'm going into the village for a walk.'

Jon looked at his watch. 'Damn! I'd come with you, but I'm waiting for a delivery.'

'Ah well,' she said, secretly glad. A walk by herself would give her a chance to get her thoughts in order. 'Maybe we can head to the pub some other time?'

Jon raised his eyebrows and smiled. 'Sure, that'd be grand!'

Oops, in her haste to make it sound like she wasn't

being rude, she'd inadvertently managed to ask him out.

'Don't look so worried,' Jon laughed, though it came out in a bit of a huff. 'No one will think anything of it, the pub's a bit like the community living room here anyway!'

'I'm not worried!' she said quickly.

'No. Just a bit frazzled maybe,' he said. 'Enjoy your walk. The craft centre should be open if you wanted to poke around, and the pub does excellent takeaway coffees these days.'

'See you later, then… or tomorrow, I guess?'

'Yep! And if you need anything, always feel free just to hammer on my door.'

~

Emmy took a long, slow breath deep into her lungs and held it there a few seconds before blowing it out. The air was sweet with the scent of spring flowers and, though there was a light breeze, warmth was creeping into the spring sunshine now.

She set off down the lane towards the humpback bridges, already feeling better. It was almost as though she'd become so used to feeling anxious over the past few months that it had become her default setting, even when there was nothing around her to get worked up about. She rolled her shoulders, trying to force her muscles to relax and let go a bit. She wasn't going to waste any more time letting thoughts of Chris or anything else from the past drag her down. This was her new start, and she was going to enjoy every second of it.

First, she was going to take Jon's advice and investigate the craft centre, and then she planned to head into the pub and kick her holiday off in style with a celebratory glass of pink wine. She winced momentarily, remembering how much Chris had taken the piss out of her for calling it pink wine.

It's called Rosaaaaay, Em, Rosaaaaaaay.

Git. And there he was again - just two seconds after she'd banished him. She huffed and shook her head. She could do better than this!

Emmy wandered through the heart of the village, peering over low hedges at the picturesque cottages and front gardens, alive with the colours of spring. In fact, the entire village seemed to have been painted by someone with a fondness for sunshine yellow. Daffodils of all shapes and sizes bobbed their cheery trumpets at her from every garden and bank, from the tiny dwarf varieties peeping out of the top of strategically placed planters to the classic whoppers standing proudly in the hedges.

Emmy loved daffodils. Marjorie would never have them in the shop because she thought they were common. Emmy thought they were beautiful, and the easiest way to bring a smile to anyone's face.

Her heart squeezed with joy as she reached the

pretty village square and memories of long summer visits came flooding back. She could almost feel Grandad Jim's hand in hers as he whispered *fancy a glass of coke, Emmy-Lou?* before leading her into the cosy pub to sit on a high stool at the bar. There she'd be fussed over by every single villager while she tucked into a bag of salt and vinegar crisps and sipped a glass of icy Coca-Cola through a straw, while her grandad chatted about gardening and the weather.

Of course, the village had been a little bit different then - though not by much. The pub still looked very much the same, although it had been treated to a new thatch and coat of paint recently and, of course, the church was still the same beautiful building she remembered from all those childhood carol services. Next door to it, however, instead of the ramshackle row of disused stables, an intricately woven willow archway opened invitingly onto the cobbles beyond, and a beautifully carved wooden sign announced that she had reached the Craft Centre.

Emmy headed under the arch and gasped in delight at the two rows of pretty shops and studios that faced each other across the cobbles. She would have loved this as a kid. Hell, she loved the look of it now!

She walked all the way to the far end of the units, looking this way and that, trying to take everything in at once. A couple of the places were closed, but as it was a random Wednesday in March, she wasn't that surprised. In fact, it was amazing that any of them were open.

She drew near to one of the closed shops and stared in awe at the window display. A female mannequin - decked out in a tartan pinafore dress, knee-high boots and a fluffy navy beret - was walking a dog-sized unicorn across a meadow dotted with flowers. On closer inspection, the field was a roll of cleverly positioned astroturf, dotted with dozens of flower-brooches.

Emmy grinned and shook her head. It was outrageous - fun and quirky, but at the same time, very clever because you instantly wanted to be this girl, walking her pet unicorn. Her eyes trailed across the flower brooches again and came to rest on a beautiful iris - yellow and purple stones twinkling on a bed of green enamel leaves. Uh oh, she was a goner! Irises were her favourite. What a shame the place was closed! Ah well, it gave her the perfect excuse to come back.

She pottered down to the next shop and peered through the door just as the woman inside looked up from her work and caught her eye.

'Hey! Come on in,' she called cheerily. She was perched on a wooden stool with a half-completed woven-willow creation balanced in front of her, a loose, whippy end in one hand.

Emmy returned her grin and stepped into what felt strangely like an indoor forest. Leaning on the walls all the way around the room were massive bundles of willow ready for weaving.

'I'm Amber,' said the girl with a warm smile. Her cropped, blond hair stood on end where she'd clearly run her fingers through it while she'd been working, and her bright yellow jumper made her look a bit like another daffodil.

'I'm Emmy. This place is amazing,' she said, tearing her eyes away from Amber to look around the studio. There were dozens of baskets hanging from the ceiling as well as various little panels and wigwams that would be perfect additions to a cottage garden. But the thing that really took her breath away was a life-sized woven carthorse that took up most of the back of the studio. Emmy's mouth dropped open and she just stood and stared.

Amber laughed. 'Yeah - he tends to have that effect quite often.'

'You *made* that?' she breathed, taking a couple of steps towards it for a closer look. She reached out a hand as if to touch it, but quickly pulled back before her inner-naughty-toddler got her into trouble.

'Oh, go ahead - he's very strong. And yes - made by my own not-so-fair hands.'

Emmy stroked her palm down the woven willow flanks, marvelling at the hours that must have gone into this piece.

'Is he for sale?' She asked curiously. There was no doubt that this massive sculpture was a work of art but she couldn't imagine that many people could house a life-sized cart-horse in their home.

'Why, you interested?' Amber smirked at her and then continued to wrap the withy she had in her hands in a spiral around the top of the wigwam in front of her.

'I... erm... I...' Emmy stuttered.

Amber chuckled. 'I'm pulling your leg, don't worry! Anyway - he's not for sale. He is a special commission for one of the show gardens at this year's Chelsea Flower Show.'

'Wow - that's incredible!' said Emmy, turning to stare at Amber with something she was sure looked a little bit like star-struck wonder. Not at all cool, but she didn't care. Emmy watched the Chelsea Flower Show every year without fail. She adored it.

'You a fan, huh?' asked Amber, curiously.

Emmy nodded. 'So much talent. So many hours of work. I mean, those show gardens...'

Amber nodded as she tied off the withy and clipped the end. 'You a gardener then?' she asked.

Emmy shook her head. 'I'm a florist. *Was* a florist,' she corrected. A pang of unexpected sadness hit her in the chest.

'*Was*? What happened?' asked Amber, grabbing a new length of willow and beginning to work it in and out of the uprights.

'I walked out of my job. The place was awful.'

'Fair enough.'

'Yeah, time to figure out something new,' she said, fingering a little woven heart that was hanging from the wall on a length of ribbon.

'Hmmm,' said Amber, stopping briefly to look at her. 'Maybe you don't need to find something new - just a different way of doing what you were already doing.'

Emmy raised her eyebrows. Was this girl a mind-reader?

'I'm sorry!' said Amber, a wry smile on her face. 'You come for a nice, quiet visit to the village and get a bunch of unwanted advice from a complete stranger.'

Emmy shook her head quickly. 'Actually, no...'

'To which part?' laughed Amber.

'I'm not visiting, I've just moved here.'

'Oooh!' squealed Amber, 'that's so exciting. Where are you living?'

'Do you know Ali Cunningham?'

'Of course!'

'I'm her niece. I'm looking after her place while she's in Australia for three months.'

'Ah, lucky you getting to stay in Dragonfly Cottage - I love that place.'

'It *is* beautiful. It was like my second home when I was growing up.'

'I thought that Jon bloke was staying there though?'

Emmy shook her head. 'He's still living in the caravan on the paddock over the road.' She didn't really want to go into it any more than that - especially as it looked like it was her fault that he'd had to change his plans.

'And you get to live right next door to the village's mystery man!' said Amber, a definite twinkle in her eye.

'What do you mean? I thought Jon had lived here for quite a while?'

'Oh, he has! But… well, he's quite private. I don't know much about him - and that's not an easy thing to manage in a village like this!'

'I can imagine!' laughed Emmy.

'He seems really nice. I know he's helped Sue out up at the allotments a couple of times, but she hasn't really told me much about him. I bet he must be missing Ali though, they spent quite a bit of time together I think.'

'Yeah. He does seem nice,' said Emmy, desperate to change the subject. She could feel her cheeks warming up again.

'I've got to say, I'm quite jealous that he gets to wake up to that beautiful field every morning.' She sighed. 'I wish I could have just a corner of that place to plant a willow crop of my own.'

'Oh - do you buy it in then?' asked Emmy, jumping gratefully onto the change of subject.

Amber nodded. 'Not ideal - I'd love to grow my own, and experiment different colours and varieties, but I can't afford a piece of land around here - it's so expensive. That's the dream though.'

'Well, maybe after Chelsea!' said Emmy warmly.

Amber sighed and gave a dreamy smile. 'Now that would be a dream come true.'

'It will. Just you wait!'

'Thank you, Emmy. I'm glad you're going to be around for a while. You're good for my ego,' laughed Amber.

CHAPTER 6

It had taken all of Emmy's willpower to tear herself away from Amber's studio. It was impossible not to like her - she exuded warmth and energy and a slight hint of mayhem that Emmy found addictive. She suspected that she may well be in the early throes of an epic girl-crush and finally decided to get out of there before she managed to embarrass herself.

She'd stuck her head into the art gallery next door and had met a lovely woman called Eve who was the polar opposite of Amber in both looks and demeanour. Her long, dark hair, shot through with strands of silver, was pulled into a soft plait over one shoulder. She'd seemed pretty shy and had kept her large, dark eyes trained on the oil painting on her easel while Emmy had looked around, again marvelling at the insane amount of talent on display.

After thanking Eve, Emmy decided to call it quits for the afternoon. She could have happily whiled away the rest of the day there, but there would be plenty of time to visit again over the next few months. Right now, that celebratory glass of wine was calling.

Emmy blinked a couple of times as she pushed her way through the door of the pub and waited for her eyes to get accustomed to the low lighting of the bar. Being late afternoon on a random Wednesday in March, the place was pretty quiet apart from a small gathering around a table at the far end of the room and an elderly woman over by the fireplace, who looked to be doing a crossword.

'Can I help you?'

The voice came from somewhere near the bar, but as Emmy peered over, she couldn't see anyone.

'Erm … hello?' she said, approaching slowly, wondering if she'd been mistaken.

'Hi!'

Emmy jumped as a smiling face appeared from below the bar.

'Oh … hi!' she said, grinning back.

'Sorry! I was just changing a barrel. What can I get for you?'

'A large glass of pink wine please.'

'Special occasion?' asked the girl, reaching into the fridge.

'Kind of,' replied Emmy, perching on a stool as

memories of grandad Jim flooded in again. 'I've just moved in today.'

'Into the village? Ooh, congratulations - and welcome - and yay!' said the girl, all in a jumble.

'Thanks!' said Emmy.

'Double yay for me, as it means I'm not the "new girl" around here anymore,' she laughed.

'Oh, did you move here recently?'

'Christmas. Well, officially just after Christmas. I crashed my car into the ditch on the top road the day before Christmas Eve... and basically never left!'

'You're kidding?' laughed Emmy.

'Nope! Fact one about Little Bamton - it has a way of holding you hostage. You'll see!'

'Well, I've only got my aunt's cottage for three months, but frankly, even that's a dream come true right now.'

'Oh, you must be Emmy - Ali's niece?'

Emmy couldn't help the look of surprise that crossed her face.

'Fact two about Little Bamton - everyone knows everything about everyone! I'm Caro by the way.'

'Nice to meet you. And yes, I'm Emmy. Cheers!' she took a swig of the deliciously cool, crisp wine and let out a sigh.

'So, is it true? Is Jon really staying put in that caravan?'

'Oh,' Emmy's heart fell. 'Well, yes. I mean, he did mention that he was going to stay in the cottage, but he decided to stay put when I asked to visit. Oh god, do you think I've caused some kind of issue?'

Caro shook her head, but Emmy noticed that she wasn't quite meeting her eye.

'Nah. I wouldn't worry about that. Jon's a big boy - and I think he and your aunt are pretty close. I'm sure they talked it all through. I'd just heard that he was going to be staying in Dragonfly because... well, never mind. Obviously I got it wrong.'

Emmy opened her mouth to ask for more info but quickly shut it again. She didn't really know this girl. She seemed friendly enough, but if Jon didn't want to tell her himself, it wasn't her place to pry. 'So, ah, where are you living now?' she asked instead, as Caro started to methodically polish a rack of glasses.

'I've got the flat upstairs - though I spend half my time at my boyfriend's cabin. Sam lives up on the top road.'

'Nice! Is that what brought you to Little Bamton in the first place?'

Caro laughed. 'Nope. Sam's the one who rescued me from the car after the crash.'

'So romantic!' sighed Emmy, before realising that she might be getting a little bit too personal - but Caro's eyes were twinkling.

'It really was. We were kind of thrown together over Christmas - I ended up staying at his place - and, well, here we are now.'

'And you moved here to be with him?' asked Emmy, seeing as though Caro clearly didn't mind.

'No - I moved here because I was offered a unit in the craft centre - dream come true! - and Lucy offered me a job in here. The two things go perfectly together. I normally do evenings here so that I can man my shop during the day - but she needed me to cover today. But yeah, being closer to Sam was a *definite* bonus.'

'Wait, you own one of the shops? I've just been over there - it's amazing!'

Caro nodded. 'Mine's the vintage shop. I make up-cycled accessories in there too.'

'Your window display is genius!' Emmy squealed and then realised it had come out a little bit louder than she'd intended. She clapped her hand over her mouth and glanced over her shoulder, only to lock eyes with the old lady over by the fireplace.

'Sorry!' said Emmy, raising her hand in an apologetic wave.

The woman gave her a little smile and went back to her crossword.

'Oops,' said Emmy sheepishly, turning back to Caro.

'Don't worry, Violet doesn't mind. She pops in almost every day for lunch. She's used to the place getting much rowdier than this!' Caro popped the glass she'd been polishing onto a shelf and then hefted another tray closer to her. 'And I'm glad you like the window!'

'I adore it,' said Emmy enthusiastically. 'There's a brooch that I've got my eye on.'

'One of the flower ones?' asked Caro.

Emmy nodded. 'The iris.'

Caro grinned. 'Nice choice.'

'They're my favourite. I'll just have to pop back when you're open.'

'Definitely! There's loads more inside too - that place is a bit like a tardis - much bigger inside than you'd expect. Excuse me for a mo?'

Emmy nodded and watched Caro hurry over to Violet's table. She turned back to her wine and swirled it around the glass thoughtfully. In the last hour, she'd met three amazing women who were all doing what they loved - Amber with her willow, Eve with her stunning paintings of village life and now Caro, moving here to chase what was clearly a dream of hers. They were all making it work.

By comparison, Emmy felt a bit like she'd retreated to Little Bamton to lick her wounds and regroup, rather than follow her passion and take the world by storm.

Emmy lifted her glass to her lips, but before taking a sip, she caught sight of her own reflection in the mirrored display behind the bar. Without thinking too much about it, she lifted her glass in a toast. *Cheers, Grandad.*

'Sorry about that,' said Caro, reappearing in front of her and popping some cash into the old fashioned till.

'No worries! I was completely monopolising you anyway. What do I owe you?' she asked.

'Nothing at all,' smiled Caro.

'I can't let you do that!' Emmy protested.

'It wasn't me - Violet insisted on paying for it as a "welcome back to the village" drink. She's treated you to a pack of salt and vinegar crisps too - "for old times sakes" She said she remembers you from when you were little!'

Emmy grinned and whipped around in her seat to thank her, but Violet was gone.

'That's so kind - and I didn't even get the chance to say thanks!' said Emmy.

'I'm sure you'll bump into her often enough to return the favour. She's a devil for the odd glass of tawny port,' grinned Caro. 'Like I said, she comes in here most days - I think she likes the company. She lives alone and I don't think she's got family close by - I guess it can get a bit lonely.'

Emmy nodded, and her heart twisted at the thought. She'd make sure that she did something for Violet to say thank you.

'I'd forgotten how friendly everyone is,' she said. 'It was always like that when I visited my grandad - like one massive family.'

Caro raised her eyebrows. 'You ain't seen nothing yet,' she laughed.

. . .

Emmy was still in a warm, wine-induced haze by the time she'd strolled back to Dragonfly Cottage. Pausing in the front garden, she stared around at the gorgeous array of grape hyacinths, early tulips that were just starting to get some colour, and the ubiquitous, sunny daffodils. Emmy smiled happily.

Her stomach grumbled, sounding ridiculously loud in the peaceful garden. Hmm. She wished she'd thought to go food shopping before making sure she couldn't drive anywhere by treating herself to that second glass of wine!

Thoughts of the car and its heavy contents still waiting to be lifted into the cottage put a little pin-hole puncture in her happy mood. Sod it. That would have to wait until tomorrow. Right now, all she was fit for was raiding Jon's bread supply and making herself an indecent amount of cheese on toast.

She wobbled her way towards the front door, feeling around in her pocket for the key. That's when she spotted the note hanging from a little hook under the letterbox.

Hey Emmy,

Hope you've had a fun time in the village. I've headed back to the van for the evening, so no need to worry about me appearing when you least expect it!

There's some left-over veg curry and rice for you in the

cast-iron pans on the stove - figured you haven't had the chance to shop yet.

Sleep well. Call me if you need anything. Number is on front of fridge.

Jon.

P.S hope you don't mind but I let myself into your car and moved the rest of your furniture upstairs for you.

Mind? She would dance a flippin' jig if there wasn't a very strong possibility of toppling over into one of the flower beds. Supper cooked for her and no lugging great big bookshelves upstairs while slightly pissed? Life was looking pretty fantastic. Sure, he'd been a bit of a surprise addition to her new life, but right now, she could kiss Jon.

CHAPTER 7

She could bloody well kill Jon. Emmy groaned as the pounding in her skull matched the throbbing tempo of the drill that was assaulting her ears. She grabbed her pillow and pulled it down over her head to muffle the racket.

What the hell was he doing here this early anyway? She'd been looking forward to a nice gentle morning, perhaps accompanied by a little bit of breakfast in bed before a trip out into the walled garden to see what would need to be done while she was here. Instead, she'd been rudely dragged from unconsciousness at this ungodly hour by someone who clearly had no sense of personal space, privacy or common, human decency.

They were going to have to have words. There needed to be some kind of ground rules if he was going to be in and out of her private space for the entire three months… that's if he wanted to survive those three months.

Emmy gave in, tossed the pillow away from her and grumpily struggled out of the bed. She was going to find him and make him go away until it was a nice, normal, human time of day.

The noise was so loud she thought it was coming from the bathroom, so she threw the door open - ready for a showdown - but there was no one there. Huh. She stomped to the other end of the hallway and opened the door to the little box room. No one there either.

She headed downstairs and into the living room, where the drilling seemed to triple in volume, connecting directly with her aching temples.

'Oi!' she shouted at Jon's back, as he held the drill to the wall at eye level.

Nothing. He didn't react… but then she wasn't really surprised. She could barely hear herself think, and his great big pair of ear defenders made doubly-sure he couldn't.

She wanted to go up behind him and give him a hefty poke in the back - but even in her hungover, ear-offended state, she wasn't stupid enough to sneak up on a guy wielding a power-tool, no matter how tempting it was.

Emmy backed away, stomped through to the kitchen and flicked the kettle on. If she had to be up and had to do battle, she may as well make sure that she was sufficiently caffeinated for the job.

As the water started its comforting rumble, she leant against the sink and stared out into the sunny garden. It was bright out there. Ridiculously bright. Gah, she hated hangovers - how could two little (okay, humungous) glasses of wine cause quite so much misery?

She was just considering routing through the kitchen drawers in search of some paracetamol when a tap on her shoulder made her squeal and wheel around.

'What the f-'

'Good morning to you too,' Jon laughed.

The sound of the drill had been enough to drag her from the deepest depths of sleep, and yet she'd spectacularly failed to notice that it had stopped since she'd come through to the kitchen. And now Jon was laughing at her.

'Your face!' he chuckled. 'Nice jammies, by the way.'

Emmy glanced down, her anger on hold for a second as she realised that she was wearing a particularly threadbare pair of cotton PJs, covered in well-loved and mostly washed-out teddy bears. She hastily crossed her arms, suddenly very aware that she hadn't glanced in a mirror before storming downstairs, and that she'd not bothered to take off her mascara the night before either.

The temptation to try to wipe away the (possible) dribble marks and the (definite) panda-impression was massive. Instead, she glared at Jon, who was now helping himself to a mug of tea from her newly-boiled kettle.

'Want one?' he asked, waggling the box of PG Tips at her.

'No,' she huffed.

'Coffee then?'

Emmy sighed, realising that if she said no to that too, she'd look like an idiot who'd boiled the kettle for no particular reason.

'It's fine, I'll do it,' she grunted.

Jon shrugged. 'It's no problem.' He grabbed a second mug from the shelf, and then pulled out a little cafetière and proceeded to make her a pot of proper coffee. Damn the man, why did he have to go and make it so hard to stay cross with him?

'I'm guessing you made it to the pub yesterday then?' he asked with a grin, sliding the milk over to her.

'What makes you say that?' she demanded.

Jon raised his eyebrows. 'Oh, you know, the fact that you are a bit... pale and interesting... and you're still in your pyjamas.'

'Of course I'm still in my bloody pyjamas,' she said. 'I'd still be in bed, asleep, if it wasn't for you and your antisocial drilling habit.'

'Just as well me and my drill are here then, isn't it?' he said, as cool as a cucumber, taking a sip of his tea and leaning back against the counter.

'No. No, it's not,' Emmy huffed. She hated confrontation, but if they didn't have this discussion now, then this was going to get out of hand way too quickly. She had to nip it in the bud. 'Look, we need to talk. Set a few boundaries between us. I get it that you need to complete the work, but I think maybe we need some rules in place as to when.'

'I completely agree,' said Jon, nodding solemnly.

Emmy scowled at him. There was something about his twinkling eyes that indicated he wasn't taking this quite as seriously as she'd like him to.

'I'm serious!' she said, and then winced. That had come out a bit too loud, and her head was starting to recoil in shock. She had to get this over and done with so that she could take her coffee and crawl back into bed for a while.

'So am I!' said Jon. 'I mean, we can't be having this conversation every day, can we?'

Emmy nodded. Every time he said something, he threw her again.

'Right. So - I think it's fair if I ask you not to start work until nine in the morning?'

Jon nodded. 'I normally start at eight-thirty, but nine would be okay.'

'Okay, great. So - if you could... come back?'

'You've lost me?' he said.

'After nine.'

Jon's sudden laughter came out in a snort. 'Emmy?'

She scowled at him again. It was way too early for whatever game this was. 'What?' she spat.

Jon took two steps towards her. To her surprise, he

placed a hand on each of her shoulders. What on earth? Was he going to kiss her? No! She hadn't brushed her teeth yet. And then there was the panda impression and possible dribble to worry about...

Jon gently steered her in a circle and then pointed to the large clock on the wall.

It took the rest of the kitchen a moment to stop spinning before Emmy could focus on the clock hands.

Ah.

Okay.

Total prat alert!

'Oh.'

'Yeah.'

It was only one word, but Emmy could hear the laughter behind it. It was twenty to twelve. She'd been rudely awakened and dragged out of bed just before noon.

'I'll go and get dressed,' she said, trying to ignore Jon's shoulders, which were now shaking with barely-suppressed laughter. She picked up her coffee and headed towards the kitchen door.

'Hey, Em?'

She turned just in time to catch the little box as it flew towards her. She looked down to find that she was clutching a pack of paracetamol.

∼

SPRING FLOWERS AND APRIL SHOWERS

By the time she'd forced down the pills, made use of Ali's snazzy, newly-installed waterfall shower and generally transformed herself back into a functioning human being, Jon and his drill were firmly back in action. The hangover that had started to recede into the background while she'd been enjoying the warm jets of water took a couple of steps forward again.

Emmy quickly realised that, if she was going to keep her sanity, she was going to have to figure out a way to be out of the cottage while a lot of this work was happening. Given that she didn't have a job to go to and didn't really know anyone yet, that could be easier said than done.

She hurried back down to the kitchen, gasping as the noise intensified. What on earth was he doing in there anyway?! She quickly made herself a stack of buttery toast and another strong cup of coffee and decided to retreat out into the walled garden.

As soon as she stepped out of the cottage's back door and into the conservatory that Ali had had installed right the way along the back of the building, she breathed a sigh of relief. The sound of the drill disappeared into the background.

She stared around, admiring this new addition to the cottage. When she was a kid, this had been a spider-infested lean-to that had housed the woodpile, her Nan's chutney and jam stash and all the bits and bobs that hadn't fit into the house or Grandad Jim's potting shed. Ali had described the new addition as a "conservatory" but in reality, it was more like a Victorian orangery. There wasn't any PVC in sight. This was built from a mixture of carved wood, wrought iron and glass. It was absolutely stunning - and completely in character with the old cottage and the garden beyond.

The slate flagstones should make the space feel cold, but Ali had scattered brightly coloured rugs across the floor, just like the ones in the living room. There was a squashy sofa and a couple of armchairs at one end, and at the other, Ali had turned the space into more of a potting shed - proving beyond all doubt that it wasn't just Emmy who'd inherited Grandad Jim's love of gardening and plants.

Ali's prized gardening tools were hanging from hooks set along the back wall, clean and well maintained, and not a prong out of place. Below them stood a sturdy pine table, along the back of which stood a range of seed trays and pots, waiting to be filled with compost, seeds and cuttings. Emmy peeped underneath the table and spotted bags of seed and potting compost, stacked neatly in type and ready for use.

Over at the far end of the space stood a propagator - and the windowsills all the way around the room held various trays and pots - some with bare compost, some with bulbs peeking out and others with tiny little geranium plants that her aunt had over-wintered in here. These were now her responsibility, and she sighed happily. She couldn't believe that this was her home for the next three months. It was going to be *so* hard to move out when Ali came back!

Yes. This would be her sanctuary while Jon got on with all the work he'd promised Ali. She could easily stay out from under his feet out here - and, maybe more importantly, not go slowly mad with all the noise!

She turned and wandered over towards the double doors that opened out into the large walled garden, sipping her coffee and munching on a piece of toast. Her eyes settled on yet more cheerful daffodils as the spring sunshine touched their heads.

The one thing that bothered Emmy about this new space was that, as well-organised and clearly loved as all of Ali's tools were, she couldn't see any of Grandad Jim's familiar tools amongst them. Surely Ali wouldn't have thrown them away? The thought made Emmy inexpressibly sad for a moment until her eyes fell on Grandad Jim's potting shed at the end of the garden. Juggling her toast and coffee, she opened up the double doors and took in a deep breath of fresh spring air as it rushed into the room. It was time to revisit the past.

CHAPTER 8

It was the smell that hit her first. The warm woody scent of the shed mixed with soil, lavender... and she could swear that she could detect a hint Grandad Jim's Old Spice aftershave. She smiled as she remembered the delight on his face when she told him he smelled like Chelsea Buns.

Emmy opened the door of the shed wider, the hinges working so noiselessly that she guessed that she wasn't the only one who'd ventured here recently in search of happy memories.

Grandad Jim's potting shed had barely changed since she was a little girl. There, in front of the windows, was the bench where they'd sat side by side - breaking up compost, sifting it between their fingers into trays, and scattering the flower seeds that were the key ingredient to the magic they both loved so much.

On the wall behind the bench hung his hand tools,

favourite gardening gloves, a beautiful old wooden soil sieve, a little basket, and a framed photograph. She took a step forward for a closer look, and a smile spread across her face even as tears prickled in her eyes. It was a photograph of Grandad Jim and herself - around the age of six - both grinning at the camera from the wooden stools at the bench. They each had a seed tray in front of them, a pile of compost and a tin mug of tea. She could just see the old, yellow wireless at the back of the bench, that surely meant that they would have been listening to BBC Radio 4.

Here it was. Physical evidence that she'd spent some of her happiest moments here with Grandad Jim, learning everything she could about growing flowers. She'd always loved the magic of annuals best - springing from seed to flower and back to seed in a single season. But that hadn't stopped her from learning as much as she could about all the other plants too.

Emmy reached out and stroked a finger across the gardening gloves, wishing she could spend one more hour out here with her grandad. She'd kept coming to visit him as she grew up, spending hours out here with him as a teen - wanting to comfort him after her Nan had died. She just wished she'd continued to visit as regularly in those last, precious years. But she'd been consumed with trying to be a grown-up, trying to make her way in the world and be everything Chris had wanted her to be. Grandad Jim had always said her life should be filled with flowers - and she couldn't help but feel like she'd let him down.

Reaching up, Emmy gently unhooked the little basket, hand-fork and trowel from their hooks. It was time to start setting things right.

~

'Interesting hangover cure!'

Jon's voice made Emmy jump. She'd been so lost in her own happy world as she'd worked over the surface of one of the flower beds. Now, as she straightened up, she realised how stiff she was from kneeling and leaning at an awkward angle for what must have been at least an hour.

She stretched her arms over her head and winced slightly as her spine gave off a cacophony of little snaps and cracks.

'Might have cured my hangover, but not sure about my back,' she laughed.

'Nice job!' he said, admiring the border. 'I know Ali said you'd be keeping an eye on the garden, but this is definitely going above and beyond the call of duty. Especially as it's only your second day here!'

Emmy shrugged. 'It's lovely out here. I like being around plants.'

'Oh, wow! Did you do those?!'

Jon's eyes were on the basket which sat next to her on the path. In it lay a bouquet she'd put together as she'd wandered around the garden. Several daffodils had keeled over, and rather than leaving them to the mercy of the slugs, Emmy had picked them with the idea of bringing them indoors to brighten up her bedroom.

As she'd pottered and snipped, her fingers had unconsciously formed them into a bouquet worthy of a bridal magazine. She'd purloined bits of greenery - a few sprigs of eucalyptus from the low branches at the bottom of the garden, and some trailing ivy she'd yanked out of the borders. She'd tied the whole thing together with some of Grandad Jim's green garden twine from the shed.

'You made this?' he asked again, leaning down to pick up the bunch for a closer look.

Emmy nodded, feeling slightly defensive. 'I didn't cut any of the good ones, just the flowers that had fallen over.'

'It's amazing!' he said. 'You should do this for a living.'

'I do… did,' she said.

'Oh - I didn't know that you're a florist.' He gently placed the flowers back into the basket.

'I'm not anymore. My old boss wasn't quite as generous with her praise as you are.'

Jon frowned. 'She sounds like an arse.'

Emmy shrugged. 'Just old fashioned. She liked things as she liked them if you know what I mean? To begin with, I was just grateful for the job and the chance to learn.'

'To begin with?'

'After several years of being reminded that you're not good enough, you get a bit fed up with hearing it.'

'So is that why you're here? Change of job?'

'Partly,' she said, scraping the last of the weeds into a little heap and popping them into a bucket. 'I had to let my flat go after splitting up with Chris - and without the job, there was nothing keeping me in Bristol.'

'But why Little Bamton?' he asked curiously.

She stood up slowly. 'Well, this!' she said, gesturing to the open potting shed. 'I'd lost touch with who I really was. This is where I was always happiest, and I needed to be surrounded by all those memories again. This is where I was always accepted for being me. Mum, Aunty Ali, Nan, Grandad Jim. They all loved me for who I was and never tried to change me.' Emmy paused as her voice cracked. She couldn't believe she was pouring all this out to a relative stranger.

Jon nodded, his face serious. 'You know,' he said, 'you're really lucky to have somewhere as special as this to come back to.'

'How about you?' asked Emmy. 'Do you still visit your family home?'

Jon shook his head, and she noticed his jaw clench briefly before he answered her.

'No. I moved around a lot as a kid - so there's nowhere, in particular, I count as home.' He stopped and cleared his throat. 'So - are you going to look for more floristry work around here?' he asked, abruptly changing the subject.

Emmy shook her head. 'No one would have me. I don't have any qualifications. Like Marjorie always said - I wasn't anything more than a glorified Saturday girl.'

Jon reached out and caught her arm gently with his hand. 'These say otherwise,' he said, pointing at her bunch of flowers. 'Do you still enjoy it?'

Emmy tilted her head and thought for a moment. No - she'd come to hate creating the monstrosities Marjorie had insisted on selling in *Daisy Days*. But on the other hand, when she'd managed to sneak one of her own hand-tied creations to a favourite customer, she'd loved it. There was nothing quite like choosing the perfect flowers for someone. She loved balancing the colours, creating highlights, binding it all together into something that was a celebration - of life, love, or friendship.

'I do,' she said at last. 'I mean, *Daisy Days* was always just a job, you know? A way to earn money. And working for Marjorie was definitely something to put up with rather than to enjoy. But the flowers? Yes - the flowers I love. I always have done.'

'So - maybe that bit's worth holding on to?'

Emmy nodded thoughtfully. 'There's a lot I don't like about commercial floristry... a lot I'd like to do differently. Seasonal, local flowers, sustainably grown -

none of the chemicals they're drowned in so that they can be shipped halfway around the world!'

'It sounds like you have a plan brewing?!' said Jon with a grin.

'Maybe...' said Emmy, then shook her head. 'Anyway, how do you fancy a cuppa?'

'Good call! I came out here to see if you wanted one anyway.'

'Great. I'll be in in a second, I just want to put everything away first.'

Jon gave her a quick thumbs-up and, much to Emmy's relief, headed back down the path towards the house. Her brain seemed to be whirring into action, and she wanted to take a second to process everything.

~

'Hey, you don't happen to know where Violet lives do you?' she asked as soon as she joined Jon in the kitchen, popping the bunch of flowers into a vase full of cold water before washing her hands and rummaging in the cupboard for his biscuit stash. She really did need to go shopping soon!

'Of course - she's in that lovely little row of cottages on the main road through towards the village square. Meadow Row? She's got the bright pink front door - though I can't remember what number that one is. Why?'

'Oh - I just thought I'd drop the flowers over for her to say thanks for buying me a drink last night.'

'Well, best of luck with that. I'm sure she's lovely, but she scares me witless!' laughed Jon. 'You know, while you're out and about, you should pop over and take a look at the paddock,' he said, leaning against the counter, munching on a ginger nut. 'You've not been over there yet, have you?'

Emmy shook her head. 'Ali said that it pretty much looks after itself - and you'd tell me if there's a problem, wouldn't you?'

'Of course. I was just thinking you might like it - it's not just bare grass like it used to be. There are some gorgeous young trees and shrubs growing down near the edge of the stream. Ali's planted willows, hazel, a couple of holly bushes - and there are all sorts of bulbs planted along the banks too. The daffs are up already - but there are plenty more to come.'

'I didn't realise…' said Emmy, thinking of the empty expanse of green she remembered from childhood as she sloshed boiling water onto a couple of teabags. 'You sure you wouldn't mind me going over there?'

'Why would I?' said Jon, surprised. 'It's not my field. I've got the caravan over in one corner - but it's at least an acre. I thought going over there might help you get your head straightened out a bit.'

'What's that supposed to mean?' Emmy snapped, pausing to glare at him.

'Nothing! I…'

'No, tell me! What did you mean?' she said, her voice cold. 'That I'm not thinking straight? That any plans I come up with are going to fail? That I should just grow up?'

Emmy was breathing heavily now. Where the hell had that come from? It might be Jon standing in front of her, but there was no doubt in her mind that it was Chris that she'd just been ranting at.

'I just thought it might help clear the tail-end of your hangover, that's all,' he said evenly.

Emmy let her shoulders drop. 'I'm sorry.'

Damn bloody Chris. This is what came from months and months of having to defend herself from his constant, snide digs at her. She was always jumping to conclusions about what people meant. She'd assumed that Jon was having a go at her when the poor bloke was just trying to be nice.

'Here,' she said, handing him his tea.

'Cheers. Right. I'll… get out of your way then.' Jon turned and headed back towards the living room.

The word "retreat" popped into Emmy's head as she watched him go, and she felt awful. Since when had she turned from an easy-going, joke-loving, laid-back kind of person to this touchy, snappy crocodile? Seems she needed this break even more than she'd realised.

CHAPTER 9

Emmy grabbed the bunch of flowers from the vase, hastily wrapped a couple of sheets of kitchen roll around the bottom to stop them dripping and then headed towards the front door. She avoided looking into the living room on her way past in case she accidentally made eye contact with Jon.

The cheerful golden trumpets in the front garden didn't have the same effect on her as they had the day before. For some reason, her exchange with Jon seemed to have undone the calm that had descended on her out in the garden and had stirred everything up again. She was worried about not having a job and she was angry that Chris was still having an effect on her life, even though he was no longer a part of it.

Emmy quickly shook her head, trying to force the worries aside. She'd drop the flowers around to Violet, then have a look at the paddock too.

She paused as she reached the first bridge and stared down at the stream as it meandered its way underneath her. What had Grandad Jim always said to her when she was sad or cross?

Give it to the water, Emmy-Lou, and let it wash all your cares away.

Reaching into her pocket, Emmy felt around until her fingers closed around a coin. Drawing it out, she saw that it was just a penny... but that would do for what she wanted it for. She held it tightly in her hand for a minute, and let all of the fear and anxiety about leaving her job, and the sadness and anger about what had happened with Chris course through her.

She tightened her grip so that the edges of the coin pressed into her skin. She closed her eyes. This was it. She was going to let it all go.

Opening her eyes again, Emmy held her hand out over the stone wall, and let the coin drop into the water.

'Strange place for making wishes, isn't it?'

The voice behind her made Emmy jump, and she was glad of the sturdy, dry stone wall of the bridge otherwise she might have followed the penny down into the water. She whipped around and came face to face with Violet.

'Not so much a wish - more a letting-go,' said Emmy, hoping Violet couldn't hear how loud her heart was thudding.

Violet raised her eyebrows and stared at her hard for a minute. 'Well, in that case, it's the perfect place.'

Emmy smiled at her.

'So, that's what brought you back at last, is it - bad break-up?' demanded Violet, her frank, piercing blue eyes capturing Emmy's.

Emmy's smile dropped. So much for a peaceful walk and a symbolic new start. It looked as though she was in for something more like an interrogation. Violet's eyes seemed to be demanding an answer from her though, so she nodded.

'Partly that, partly being out of a job and feeling a bit lost.' She paused and picked up the flowers from the wall. 'I was just coming to see you, actually. These are for you - to say thank you for the drink last night.' Emmy held them out to her.

Violet's face softened for a second as she reached out and took them, before setting off again in the direction of the village, beckoning for Emmy to join her.

Emmy fell into step next to the sprightly older woman - it was as much as she could do to keep up with her as she beetled along.

'You know you're not really lost, don't you, dear?' she said, peeping sideways at Emmy. 'You found your way back here, just like your Grandad Jim always said you would. He was so proud of you and so sure you'd find your way back home. And Little Bamton has a habit of putting people back on the right path. Sometimes it can take a little while, but it always seems to manage it somehow.'

Emmy laughed. 'It's always been a special place.'

'Yes, the place is lovely, but take it from me - after long years of figuring out my own messes, it's people who make or break a place. Little Bamton seems to gather waifs and strays and turns them all into one large family.'

'I think that's why my aunt has always loved it so much!' said Emmy.

Violet huffed a little at that, and Emmy cast a quick glance at her.

'She did love it, but she had a hard time of it, helping to look after your nan, and then nursing your Grandad Jim at the end. I think it was high time for Ali to go and have some adventures. She deserves them.'

'But she still loves it here!'

'Oh, I don't doubt that, dear, I just don't think it'll be her home again. It's your turn now.'

'Well, it's definitely my turn for the next three months, anyway,' Emmy said. She wondered where all this was coming from. Ali had never given her the slightest indication that her visit to Australia was anything more than just a holiday. Perhaps Violet had the wrong end of the stick, or maybe this was just a case of the usual village gossip.

'This is me,' said Violet abruptly, pushing open her gate and turning off onto her garden path.

'What a gorgeous garden,' said Emmy, gazing over the box hedge.

'Just you wait until spring gets underway properly - then you'll see some flowers!'

'I can't wait,' said Emmy. 'I think cottage gardens are my favourite - even more than the big, formal gardens. You can't beat that mix of plants - so much colour and texture.'

'Are you a gardener then?' asked Violet. 'Your grandad always said you'd end up working with plants.'

Emmy shook her head. 'Florist.'

'One of those fancy ones, no doubt - all imported orchids and such?'

Emmy shook her head. 'I actually prefer seasonal and British, if it's up to me.'

'Hm. Well, maybe we'll get on then,' said Violet, an approving tone in her voice. 'I just wish there was somewhere you could buy flowers like that these days! Now then, if you'll excuse me, it's time for my breakfast.'

Emmy just managed to squeak out a surprised goodbye before Violet beetled up the garden path and disappeared behind the bright pink front door.

Emmy took a couple of steps, as if to continue her walk towards the village square, then turned back to look at Violet's garden again. Something about it and the old lady's words had stirred up an idea - but it was like a wisp of mist hovering over the little stream - something that she couldn't quite catch hold of yet.

She peered at the nodding heads of the daffodils, a small patch of miniature irises that were nearly over, and an array of shoots that promised tulips galore. Lavender and rosemary bushes stood sentinel under the cottage windows, still half asleep after the long winter. The well-pruned rose bushes were just starting to push out their lush new shoots.

This was a classic, old fashioned cottage garden - and she had no doubt that it would be full to bursting with all the blooms she most enjoyed working with in just a few weeks.

There it was again - a tingle of inspiration. She could almost feel Grandad Jim standing at her elbow, giving her a nudge. Emmy took in a deep breath and let it out slowly.

Then she realised that she was standing stock still, staring into Violet's garden like some creepy creeperson. Perhaps it was time to move on before the neighbourhood watch thought they had trouble on their hands.

∼

When she got back to Dragonfly Cottage, Emmy headed straight across the lane towards the paddock's gate. She quickly scaled it and jumped down the other side, landing lightly on the soft, springy grass.

Off to her right, tucked in behind the hedge, stood Jon's caravan. She raised her eyebrows as she stared at it. She'd been expecting something more akin to a park home, but this was a tiny thing. It was more like the ones she'd seen on the dual carriageway, heading to Cornwall for a weekend away. Only, this one didn't look like it would hold together for more than about a minute if anyone dared to try towing it anywhere. It was ancient, green with algae on top, and looked like a stiff gust of wind might cause it to collapse.

A wave of guilt washed over her. It was her fault that he was still living out here rather than in the cosy cottage. She sighed. There wasn't anything she could do about that right now.

Give him his due, Jon had done his best to prettify his home. There were low, woven willow panels hammered into the ground around it, marking out a tiny patch of private outdoor space. She could also glimpse a bunch of tubs - some with the ubiquitous yellow daffs, and others looking like they'd just been sown - the compost in them was still bare. She could just make out little white labels in each pot and itched to pop over and see what Jon was going to grow. But common sense prevailed. She'd already managed to piss him off once today - checking out his plant pots would definitely classify as snooping.

Emmy tore her eyes away from Jon's corner, and she looked out across the rest of the paddock. It really was glorious.

The bank that ran down from the hedge-line parallel to the lane was covered with yellow blooms.

The hedgerow itself was a mixture of hazel and hawthorn. She could only imagine that when May rolled around, it would be dotted with the fragrant, pinky-white sprays of delicate flowers that she loved so much.

The far side of the field sloped gently downwards, and she headed in that direction, drawn by the sounds of trickling water before she even spotted the little stream.

She knew she was probably being ridiculous, but as she made her way to the water's edge, she couldn't help thinking how friendly it seemed. It was only a couple of meters wide, and wasn't particularly deep, other than where the flow had carved out deeper pools here and there.

As she gazed, transfixed by the miniature waterfalls and whirlpools created by the rocks that formed the riverbed, Emmy spotted a couple of tiny fish darting this way and that in the clear water.

She took in a deep lungful of the fresh, spring air. It smelled of grass and flowers and new beginnings. She let the sound of the water wash over her as she revelled in the slight ache in her muscles from the little bit of gardening she'd done. She already felt more like herself.

Emmy turned and headed back out into the centre of the field. The grass was tussocky and wild at the moment, but Emmy could only imagine that come summer, it would be knee-high and dotted with all sorts of wildflowers if it was left to grow.

It always came back to flowers for her, didn't it? Standing here in the spring sunshine, she felt that nudge at her elbow again, as if Grandad Jim was prompting her.

There it was. She knew why she was here, and what she wanted to do. Now all she needed were the balls to go for it.

CHAPTER 10

Emmy shot bolt upright in the bed. Her heart was racing and her forehead was sweaty. It was the same stupid nightmare she'd had every single night since her walk over in the paddock.

She took a deep breath and reached for her water glass on the nightstand, trying to calm her heart rate down. She was a grown woman for heaven's sakes - she shouldn't be frightened by stress-dreams involving her old boss.

Emmy shuddered, unable to shake the feeling of hopelessness that came with the dream, where she was working to create enough displays for a huge wedding, but every time she finished a piece, a strangely misshapen Marjorie - her oversized head crowned with a Duchess basket - would come along behind her and throw her work in the bin. Then she'd open her mouth and cough up one of the designs from the *Daisy*

Days catalogue which would land with a *thump thump thump* in front of her.

It wasn't remotely scary when she thought about it rationally, but her sleeping brain was clearly having a hard time keeping things rational at the moment.

Emmy sipped her water and sighed. It was Saturday, which meant no Jon, which also meant she'd planned on having a lie-in. No such luck! She needed coffee. Chucking the bedclothes aside, Emmy grabbed her clothes from the chair and pulled on her jeans, tee shirt and a warm hoodie before heading downstairs.

She padded through to the kitchen and flicked the kettle on, yawning widely. The only way she was going to function today was with a great deal of caffeine.

A loud *meow* at her feet made her jump as Charlie appeared, demanding food.

'Dude - me first, then it's your turn!' she mumbled.

Charlie started to wind his way around her ankles again, so she bent over and gingerly tickled him behind the ears. He put up with it for a couple of seconds before retreating and staring at her intently.

'Okay, okay. Breakfast. I get it!'

Emmy quickly dished out Charlie's stinky food - which he proceeded to guzzle while she poured herself some wake-up juice and flopped down in one of the wooden chairs at the table. She was exhausted. She could really do with a couple of nights sleep minus another instalment of Marjorie and her amazing 1980s flower vomit. The dark circles under her eyes were coming along nicely. The dreams, combined with the on-going cool-but-polite stand-off she had going with Jon following her crocodile-impersonation, meant that she was feeling far from chilled. Especially given that every inch of her fizzed with excitement every time he was near. Damn it, this break was meant to help her get herself sorted out, not make things worse!

Emmy sipped her coffee gratefully. She seemed to be at some kind of strange impasse. She was so excited about her new plans, but every time she sat down to work on them properly, she just ended up with pages full of flowery doodles in her notebook, and nights filled with anxiety dreams. What she really needed was someone to talk to. She'd felt so sure her plan could work, but with the nightmarish visions of Marjorie, and their inevitable link to her life with Chris back in Bristol, everything felt really jumbled.

'Emmy?'

Jon's voice out in the hallway made her jump. What the hell was he doing here? She flushed uncomfortably. She turned in her chair to greet him as naturally as she could, considering their current status could only be described as *frosty*.

'Oh, hey Jon,' she croaked.

'Sorry to barge in. I've just picked up a couple of parts for Monday's work and wanted to stash them in the corner of the living room if you don't mind?'

Emmy pushed her hair back behind her ears and shook her head. 'Of course - that's fine.'

'Great. Oh - and this was on the doorstep.'

He held out a large canvas shopper. Its rope handles were tied together with green ribbon, and it had a star printed on it.

'Thanks!' she said, surprised.

'No worries.' He paused a second, thrusting his hands into his jacket pockets looking uncomfortable. 'Right, I'll get out of your hair,' he said, turning to go.

'You want a coffee first?' she blurted. What should have been a simple, casual offer felt more like a momentous challenge - but she had to ask, didn't she? Obsessing about him whenever he wasn't around and then barely speaking a word to him when he was really wasn't doing her equilibrium any good at all.

Jon turned back to her and shook his head. 'Can't, sorry. I promised a mate I'd help him do a couple of tip runs today.'

'Oh, okay,' she said, her heart sinking. 'Have fun!'

'Not sure about that,' grunted Jon, as he headed back out into the hall.

Emmy forced herself to wait until Jon had finished bringing the parts in from his van before she opened the mystery shopping bag. It took every ounce of restraint she had to sit, calmly sipping coffee until he called out a gruff goodbye.

As soon as he'd gone, Emmy breathed a sigh of relief. She pulled the bag towards her carefully untied the silky ribbons to look inside.

There were five little parcels, all wrapped in

different paper. There was also a bright pink envelope, so she reached in and plucked that out first. It had her name on it in large, swirly letters. Emmy gave a little squeal, resulting in a hiss from Charlie as he shot out of the room. She chuckled guiltily and tore open the envelope and pulled out a sheet of equally bright writing paper inside.

Hey Emmy - it's Caro (from the pub?!)

I wanted to invite you to our girly book club tonight. Sorry to leave it so late - I thought I might see you at some point, but as I haven't, I thought I'd bring these around.

We meet once a month on a Saturday night at 7pm - and we rotate between our various houses. Tonight we're meeting at mine - so if you fancy it, rock up at 7pm. I'm above the pub - just look for the bright red door around the back. If you can't make it this time I'll let you know where the next one will be. And don't worry about it if you haven't read the book - it's more of an excuse for a girly gossip and a glass of wine! This month we're going back to the classics with Pride and Prejudice!

The parcels are from all of us - just little house-warming gifts.

Hope you can make it, see you soon,

Caro xxx

P.S just bring yourself - vino plonko is on me tonight!

. . .

Emmy felt like her prayers had been answered. She was someone who usually enjoyed her own company, but after spending several quiet evenings alone, after long days avoiding Jon wherever she could - she was dying for a bit of company.

She reached into the bag and took out the gifts, lining them up one-by-one on the table. One was obviously a book, meticulously wrapped in silver tissue with a thin, shimmery blue ribbon around it. Another was a bottle, wrapped in plain brown parcel paper. Then came a large Tupperware tub that wasn't wrapped. She peered inside it and spotted a massive, delicious-looking Victoria sponge. A quick look at the sticker on top said that it was sent *with love, from Lucy.*

The other two parcels were complete mysteries - one a tiny, square package wrapped in purple velvet, and the other, wrapped in handmade paper, was larger but very light. She tore into this one first and gasped in delight as a little woven-willow heart fell onto the table. It was the ornament she had been eyeballing in Amber's shop on her first day back in the village. Sure enough, there was a tag tied to the bottom with the words *love from Amber* scrawled on it in pencil.

Emmy set it aside and picked up the little square next. Carefully undoing the narrow, white ribbon, she unfolded the velvet to reveal a jewellery box. Emmy raised her eyebrows and hastily snapped open the lid. Inside, nestled on a pillow of cotton wool, was the iris brooch she'd been dribbling over in Caro's shop window.

She lay the box gently next to the wreath, and with slightly shaking fingers picked up the third parcel. She'd guessed this one right - it was a book - a lovely old Penguin Classic copy of Pride and Prejudice. Emmy smiled and flipped open the cover to read the oh-so-familiar first line when something fell out and fluttered to the floor.

She leaned down awkwardly and plucked the thick piece of paper off the floor. It was a bookmark - but not like any she'd seen before. On one side was an exquisite watercolour painting of the front door of Dragonfly Cottage - complete with the trellis arch covered in summer roses. Turning it over, Emmy saw that Eve had signed it and added her love. Emmy swallowed hard, fighting back a lump of emotion that had risen in her throat. There was so much kindness in these beautiful gifts that she felt quite overwhelmed and was suddenly very glad that she was opening them alone.

Emmy reached out to peel the paper off the bottle of wine, then laughed out loud - because the girls had obviously been talking. The wine's original label had been covered over with a handmade affair which stated boldly - *"Emmy's Pink Wine."*

Emmy couldn't help but feel a little bit nervous as she wandered through the village towards the pub. She was really looking forward to the book club meeting, and thanking everyone for their gorgeous gifts, but still… it had been a while since she'd had any proper girly time!

She carefully adjusted the basket she was carrying over the crook of her arm. As soon as she'd finished opening her gifts that morning, she knew she wanted to take them all something in return. Short of driving to the supermarket to buy something, she felt stumped for a moment. Anyway, nothing from a supermarket could ever compare with the personal touch of every single one of those packages. The answer came to her as she'd stood at the kitchen sink rinsing out her coffee cup. Flowers. Of course.

She was sure her aunt wouldn't mind her cutting a few blooms to take to her new friends.

Emmy had rooted around in the conservatory, convinced that she'd find the perfect thing. It hadn't taken her long to discover an entire box of clean, pretty jam jars. She selected five and lined them up on the potting table. Then, she'd fetched the old basket from Grandad Jim's shed and went out into the garden, where she'd helped herself to a pile of sweetly scented narcissi. Their tiny heads were made up of a disc of near-white petals and cute, dark orange trumpets. Then she added a large bunch of vibrant blue-purple grape hyacinths from a massive stone planter at the bottom of the garden. By the time she'd finished picking, it barely looked as though she'd taken any at all.

Emmy created five gorgeous little posies in the jars and finished them off by wrapping them with green garden twine from Grandad Jim's shed, adding a rustic bow as the final touch. Looking at them now, Emmy smiled. It was only something small - but she hoped they would like them.

She was at the pub before she knew it, and headed around the back as Caro had suggested. The pub itself looked like it was heaving - chatter and laughter pouring out. It looked warm and inviting. She wondered who was manning the bar if both Caro and Lucy were upstairs to talk about books!

Emmy spotted Caro's front door at the top of a set of stone stairs that ran up the back of the building. Emmy climbed up and knocked lightly. She'd barely had the chance to compose her nerves when the door was flung open.

'You came!' squealed Caro, reaching out to grab her arm and drawing into a bear-hug.

CHAPTER 11

'Thank goodness you're here!' said Caro, excitedly grabbing her by the hand and leading her through to a cosy living room. Amber and two women she didn't recognise were already relaxing with drinks in hand. 'You've turned up just in time to agree with me that Colonel Brandon has *way* more phwoar factor than Mr Darcy.'

'Oh, come *on!*' sighed Amber from her beanbag. 'Emmy has far too much taste to agree with that, don't you Em?'

'My goodness, you two - let the poor girl take her coat off first!' laughed one of the women on the couch. She guessed this must be either Lucy or Sue. She looked to Caro in the hope that she might do the honours.

'Sorry lovely! First things first - everyone, this is

Emmy. Emmy, you already know Amber, and this is Sue,' she pointed to the woman who'd just spoken, 'and Lucy, who owns the pub,' she pointed at the woman curled up next to Sue.

'Hi!' said Emmy with a grin.

'And Eve's on her way, she just texted me before you arrived - lost track of time working on her new painting.'

'What's new?' laughed Lucy.

'Shall I take your coat?' said Caro.

'Oh, erm, thanks!' Emmy awkwardly popped the basket of flowers down onto the floor and stripped off her duffel coat - which was a mercy as the room was beautifully cosy and she'd already started to brew up.

'What gorgeous flowers!' said Lucy, leaning forward to peer into her basket.

'They're for you lot!' said Emmy. 'To say thank you for my presents. That was such an amazing surprise-'

'These are for us?' asked Amber, leaning forward and taking one of the jars in her hands.

'Yep. I know they're not much, but-'

'Ooh, thanks Emmy, these are gorgeous!' said Sue as Amber passed her one.

Emmy flushed.

'Yes, thank you, lovely,' said Lucy.

'It's nothing. Thank you so much for inviting me tonight!'

'Glad you could make it at such short notice!' said

Caro, coming back into the room. 'Go on girl, grab a seat!'

Emmy sank into an empty armchair.

'So,' said Caro, flopping down into her own chair and staring at Emmy expectantly.

'So...?' asked Emmy.

'Darcy or Brandon?' demanded Caro, as the others chuckled.

'I've always been more of a Captain Wentworth fan myself,' said Emmy, a grin spreading over her face.

~

By the time Eve turned up, Emmy had a glass of pink in hand and was merrily throwing herself into the conversation - which had started with Colin Firth in a wet shirt and had quickly ended up in a heated, giggly argument about the best cinematic version of the book.

'The question is,' said Eve, unwinding her scarf and looking around at them all with a twinkle in her eye, 'did any of you actually read the book? Or has everyone just spent the week enjoying a quick refresher course courtesy of Mr Firth?'

'Shocking, what a thing to ask,' giggled Amber.

'Guilty,' grinned Lucy.

'Neither for me, I'm afraid,' said Emmy.

'I think you get a free pass this week, considering we only got the invite to you this morning!' said Eve.

'Too kind,' laughed Emmy. 'Oh, and that reminds me, these are for you.' She reached down and passed the last jar of flowers up to Eve. 'As a thank you for your gorgeous presents. I'll treasure that bookmark - it's really special.'

'Thank you,' said Eve, looking both surprised and delighted, 'that's so kind!'

'Feeling's mutual,' said Emmy, warmly.

'Alright, alright,' said Sue, shifting along the sofa so that there was room for Eve on the end. We've already discussed the book - what's next on the agenda.

Emmy's jaw dropped, but everyone else fell about laughing.

'I did warn you!' said Caro, catching the look on her face.

'I want to know more about Emmy!' said Lucy, smiling at her.

'Good call,' said Amber, turning to stare at her.

Emmy felt the blush start at her toes and wash up over her like a wave.

'You guys are too much sometimes,' said Eve. 'But yes - what do you do Emmy? I'm going to guess - florist? Anyone who can make daffodils look this chic has to be!'

Emmy smiled at her, grateful for the rescue. 'I used to be a florist.'

'Oh no, dear,' said Sue, shaking her head, 'there's no *used to be* about it.'

'Well, I left my job, so at the moment, I don't actually *do* anything.'

'And so you came here to live next to the village heart-throb!' said Amber, causing Caro to splutter her wine.

'Heart-throb?' echoed Emmy, playing for time. They had to be talking about Jon.

'Oh come on Emmy - even I have to admit that Jon would look good in a wet-shirt scene,' said Eve with a smile, her eyes twinkling.

'Even you? What's that supposed to mean?!' demanded Sue. 'A gorgeous woman like you…'

Eve laughed quietly and shook her head. 'Divorced, the wrong side of forty and about to be living alone when Davy goes to college,' she sighed, her smile wavering a moment.

'Davy's Eve's lad,' said Lucy, filling Emmy in quickly.

'Yep. My boy's eighteen already,' sighed Eve. 'And I just meant that gorgeous guys haven't been very high on my agenda recently - just like I haven't been very high on theirs either!'

'Well,' said Amber, 'don't you worry about that. With Davy off on his adventures, you'll be able to make up for lost time and dedicate yourself to all the gorgeous guys your heart desires.' She winked at Eve, who raised her glass even as she shrugged her shoulders.

'Anyway,' said Eve, 'we weren't talking about me. We were talking about Jon and Emmy.'

'There isn't a Jon and Emmy!' said Emmy, rather too quickly, her cheeks flaming.

Lucy raised her eyebrows. 'Emmy - do you *like* Jon?'

'What is this, primary school?' laughed Amber.

Emmy shrugged. 'I... I...'

'Well that clears that up then!' laughed Caro.

Emmy cleared her throat. 'Even if I did *like* him - which I'm not saying I do - I think I've already managed to cock it up,' she said glumly.

'Why?' asked Eve curiously. 'What did you do?'

'Snapped his head off,' said Emmy. 'It wasn't his fault. My ex used to pick at me all the time. Jon said something, I took it completely the wrong way and exploded. I guess I've just got to the point where I take any comment from a guy as a negative. I'm such an idiot.'

'You're definitely not an idiot,' said Lucy gently.

Eve nodded. 'Yeah, it takes a really long time to start trusting other people again after a break-up.'

'I do trust Jon!' said Emmy surprised. 'But I doubt he trusts me now. It's like I auto-snap before I realise what I'm doing.'

'Jon's a sensible lad,' said Sue, 'a really nice, genuine bloke. Just apologise and tell him what happened.'

'I apologised straight away but he's been really quiet ever since - not that I blame him!'

'Did you explain?'

Emmy shook her head and heaved a sigh. 'No. He'd just think I'm an idiot.'

'Definitely not,' said Sue, and the others all mumbled their agreement. 'Look, that lad has been through an awful lot. It's not my place to say anything - but I bet, if you can bring yourself to be open with him, he'll understand.'

Much to Emmy's relief, Amber tactfully changed the conversation to craft centre gossip. It gave her a moment to digest Sue's advice. She was right, she should just apologise again and explain what had happened. She would nip into town in the morning, grab some much-needed shopping and pick up a peace offering for him while she was at it.

'Earth to Emmy!' said Caro, smiling at her. 'You okay?'

'Oh, yeah, sorry. I was just thinking about the fact that I've really got to get some supplies in tomorrow!'

'I've got to go into town tomorrow myself - we can go together if you'd like?'

'Thanks, that'd be great.'

'Good. So are you going to be looking for work while you're here?' asked Caro. 'There's a florist in the next town over. They do nice enough stuff - but it's very - how can I put this - high design? Does that make sense?'

Lucy nodded in agreement. 'They're like pieces of abstract art. Very beautiful - but sometimes I just want to enjoy the beauty of the flowers, you know?'

Emmy nodded. This was a topic of conversation she could get behind. 'I know exactly what you mean. That was never really my style. I like seasonal flowers, hand-tied. I love playing with colours and textures - but it's about letting the flowers be the star of the show - not all the props and bits and bobs.'

'And you say you're not a florist!' laughed Sue.

'Well, technically I'm not at the moment.'

'Weren't you happy at your last place then?' asked Caro, taking a sip of wine.

Emmy sighed. 'Not by the end. I mean, to start with I learned a lot - but I was there for five years - and *Daisy Days* was a massive 1980s throwback.'

'Oooh,' said Caro, looking interested.

'No - not in the funky, vintage way you're imagining,' laughed Emmy. 'We're talking oasis heart pillows stuffed with half-dead pink carnations, edged with gypsophila.

A shudder went around the whole room, followed by quite a lot of giggling.

'So what made you leave?' asked Eve curiously.

'My boyfriend left me,' said Emmy bluntly.

They all looked a bit non-plussed, except for Lucy, who nodded. 'One big change made another one seem easier?' she asked.

'Something like that. I'd just had enough of being treated badly. Men. Jobs. I decided that I deserve more.'

'Woop!' squealed Amber, raising her glass to her.

'Hear hear,'

'Amen!'

'Good for you!'

'Anyway,' she said cautiously, 'the answer's no - I'm not going to look for a job. I've had an idea... it would be great if I could run it past you all, actually.'

The room was suddenly, eerily quiet as they all faced her, waiting for her to speak. Until Amber let out a giggle, which she hurriedly stifled.

'Sorry, sorry,' she snuffled, 'I just felt like we were on a film set or something.'

Emmy chuckled, grateful for Amber's outburst as it had let the tension out of the moment a little bit.

'Come on, girl - that's enough keeping us in suspense!' laughed Caro. 'Out with it!'

'Well, I'd really like to start selling flowers here in Little Bamton,' she said. There, it was out. Plaster ripped off in one go.

'What, you mean set up a florist?' asked Sue.

Emmy shook her head. 'No... not exactly. I don't want to buy flowers in but use local ones. Ideally, I'd like to grow my own, but I was thinking I could start small and use ones from Aunty Ali's garden,' Emmy paused, looking around at them all, trying to read their reactions.

'Well, I love the idea!' Said Lucy warmly. 'It would be amazing to be able to buy fresh flowers in the village. The allotment always has a little cart at the gate during growing season with all sorts of fruit and veg available for sale that they've grown. Is that the sort of thing you were thinking?'

'Exactly,' said Emmy, nodding. 'A couple of tables to start with, and an honesty box. Though I'm not sure where I could set them up... the cottage is a little bit too out of the way...'

'There's that little patch of grass on the corner down by the bridges. Close enough to Dragonfly to keep an eye on it and stock it up, but nicely visible for anyone heading in and out of the village,' said Sue. 'I'm not sure it belongs to anyone in particular, but you could always ask permission from the Parish Council.'

Emmy nodded thoughtfully. She knew the spot - it was visible from the road on the way into the village, and there was plenty of space to pull a car up, should anyone want to stop.

'I love this idea!' said Amber. 'You could have little treats like the ones you gave us tonight, huge bunches, simple single-flowers bunches and full-blown bouquets!'

'Do you think you'll be able to pick enough from the cottage garden to do it?' asked Caro.

'To begin with. I mean, I'll only start small - no weddings or anything insane like that - just the stall. And of course, I'd have to ask Aunty Ali's permission first,' said Emmy. 'I just hope she likes the idea!'

'I've known Ali a long time,' said Lucy. 'she's going to love the idea.'

'You really think so?'

Lucy and Sue both nodded enthusiastically.

'And you all really think this could work?' she asked nervously.

The resounding "yes" from all five of them brought tears to Emmy's eyes.

CHAPTER 12

Emmy's brain was still whirring by the time Caro dropped her off the next day. Book club had given her way too much to think about, and she'd wandered the aisles of the local supermarket half in a dream. Caro had repeatedly asked her if she was okay, and Emmy had just nodded.

She picked up her shopping bags and headed towards the cottage. As much as she liked Caro and was grateful to her for the lift, she was incredibly glad to be on her own again. Her thoughts had been a never-ending carousel of Jon and flowers, Jon and flowers, ever since the previous evening. How could she apologise to Jon? Could she really start her own flower stall? Around and around it went until she felt confused and dizzy.

Emmy had gone to town with the shopping. She'd replaced the basics they'd gone through between them, and then added in plenty of treats too. She knew she was being a bit pathetic, hoping to win him over with his favourite ginger biscuits, but it was worth a try, wasn't it?

She let herself into the mercifully quiet cottage and ferried the bags in two at a time until the kitchen table was groaning under the weight of groceries.

At last, she flopped down onto one of the kitchen chairs - only to jump as Charlie nudged her leg with his nose.

'Oh, it's you is it?' she said, peering down at him. Charlie looked back up at her with accusing eyes. Clearly, he'd been hoping to find Jon - not her. 'Sorry mate, I'm your best chance of Dreamies and chin rubs today.'

Charlie opened his mouth and gave a rusty *meow*, staring at her unblinkingly. Ah. Well. She had mentioned the magic word. She sighed, reached forward and grabbed the pack of treats from the middle of the table, and took off the clothes peg that was keeping it rolled down.

At the rustle of the packet, Charlie started to wind in and out of her feet, his purrs reaching an alarming volume, sounding a bit like Jon's drill.

'Here you go, you fickle fiend,' she laughed, shaking a couple into her palm and putting them down on the floor for him. She'd seen Jon feed them by hand to the pampered puss, but Emmy wasn't quite secure enough in their friendship to give it a try

- not to mention that she treasured her fingers too much!

Charlie hoovered up the offering in seconds and then sat back to stare at her steadily. She was pretty sure that he was attempting a spot of feline hypnosis - but she wasn't going to fall for it. No chance, no way.

'Okay mate, two more and then that's it,' she chuckled, shaking out a couple more treats and popping them down in front of him again.

Charlie crunched them down happily, and Emmy quickly got to her feet, determined not to let him play on her soft side for a second time.

She started to load some of the shopping into the almost-bare fridge. As she caught a glimpse of the garden, looking fresh and colourful in the spring sunshine, her mind wandered back to the idea of the flower cart for what must have been the three-thousandth time that morning.

There was no doubting that she could do with the income - that's if it made anything at all. Despite everyone's excitement at book club, Emmy just couldn't imagine that it would earn much. She had some savings left, but she didn't want to blow through those on some mad plan that she'd have to abandon when the time came to move on from Little Bamton. Of course... she was just planning to use a couple of tables to start with - and it wasn't as though she'd have to pay anything out for the flowers either, so her outgoings would be tiny.

Emmy let out a huge sigh as Charlie meowed at her

again, bring her back to the present with a bump. She wished she could ask Jon what he thought of the plan. Somehow, she'd really value his thoughts on the whole thing.

Hm. Jon. The other side of the coin that had been rolling around in her head since yesterday. She really did need to do something to clear the air between them, especially as her little outburst had had nothing to do with him - he'd just happened to be in the vicinity.

Emmy put her hands on her hips and stared hard at Charlie for a moment. 'What do you think, cat? Time to stop being a pussy and get on with it?'

Charlie meowed at her again and followed it up with a little hiss as he turned his back and sauntered away from her.

'Fair enough,' she laughed.

She went to the table and ferreted around for the four-pack of craft beer she'd bought as a peace-offering and then, on a whim, reached into the cupboard and brought out the Victoria sponge. She grabbed the bread knife, cut the entire cake in half, and then proceeded to lift one half onto a plate and covered it with clingfilm. There. If he couldn't be won over by beer and cake, things were way beyond mending.

Reaching for her basket, she popped the beers into one corner and then balanced the plate next to them.

'Here goes nothing.'

Her knock on the door of the caravan seemed to echo the panicked beating of her heart. Emmy wouldn't normally classify herself as a cowardy-custard, but this morning she was doing a damned good impression of one.

She stood stock-still, listening for any sounds from inside. She was sure she'd heard music on her way over here, but now there was just silence. She took in a deep breath, trying to calm her nerves. This was ridiculous - sure, she'd pissed him off a bit with her snappy comment, but it wasn't as though they hadn't seen each other at all since then. So why was she in such a state?

It was all that talk last night of him being the local heart-throb that had done it - and no matter how much she'd tried to down-play everything in front of the girls, she couldn't do the same with herself. She'd spent an indecent amount of time picturing Jon in Ali's new shower!

She knocked again, just to make sure that he really wasn't there. She guessed she could just leave the basket on the doorstep for now, though her heart sank a little bit at the idea - it didn't quite convey the apology she'd had in mind. Ah well, there was nothing for it.

She set it down and had just turned back towards the field gate when she heard the caravan door creak open behind her.

'Oh, it's you,' said Jon shortly, as she turned back to look at him.

Her apology stalled on her lips. He looked awful. His skin was pale, and his eyes red, as though he'd been rubbing at them.

'Erm, yeah,' she said, uncertainly.

'Everything okay?' he asked her, raising his eyebrows, then peering over his shoulder back into the caravan.

'Oh - yup, fine,' she followed his eyes and saw a bucket on the floor behind him. Was he ill? 'Are you okay?'

Jon nodded and looked vaguely annoyed. 'What can I do for you, Emmy?'

'Oh - right - nothing! I just wanted to let you know that I've been shopping at last - so there are plenty of supplies at the cottage - if you need anything. Thanks for letting me scrounge off you for so long,' she knew she was rambling, but she was suddenly desperate to keep him there at the door.

'Right. Great. It's fine,' he said. 'Look I'd better-'

'And these are for you,' she interrupted him before he shut the door in her face. 'To say thanks. The cake is from Lucy - but I thought you might like some.'

Jon reached out on autopilot and took the basket from her. 'Thanks.' He looked down at the beers and then back at her. 'Thanks. Look I'd better go.'

Suddenly she was looking at the closed door of the caravan again. Jon had just shut it in her face.

Well, that was that, then. She'd done her best, and he clearly wasn't interested in any kind of friendship with her - let alone any shower-related activities. She'd definitely have to put an end to her imagination wandering in that direction!

She was just heading back towards the gate, muttering to herself about rude ass-hats and regretting handing over half of Lucy's cake to someone that ungrateful when she stopped in her tracks. Her other obsession was busy elbowing her in the ribs for attention.

Flowers.

She looked around at the paddock with fresh eyes and suddenly saw it teaming with flower beds. This would be the perfect place to grow her own stock for her stall. With the right amount of planning and preparation, there was enough space here to grow every flower imaginable - more than she could ever need - even if she became some kind of highly sought-after wedding florist.

From feeling irritated and disappointed just a few seconds ago, she now felt a ridiculous surge of excitement. Her imagination was bouncing from wigwams of fragrant sweet peas to entire beds full of pom-pom dahlias, to perfumed English roses and classic lily of the valley for next year's blushing brides.

She turned on the spot, already able to see the perfect array of growing beds, enough space in between them to push a mower along to maintain them easily. Over there, she could set up a composting system, and over *there* she could treat herself to a polytunnel.

Then she caught sight of Jon's caravan, and it was like a pin had punctured her little daydream. Huh - no chance of any of that happening was there? For one thing, she was only here for a couple of months, and for another thing - the paddock simply didn't belong to her. This was her aunt's property and as her tenant, Jon probably had more rights to it than she did. No matter how fast she was falling in love with Little Bamton - it wasn't her home. She was just a visitor. Setting up a flower stall while she was here was one thing, but her own little flower farm? That was something else entirely. Something exciting… something out of reach.

Emmy set off at a fast pace back to the cottage, wanting to get out of the paddock before the images of her daydream that could never come true drove her mad.

CHAPTER 13

It had been a truly shitty day. After getting back from her disastrous attempt to make peace with Jon, she hadn't been able to settle to anything. Emmy felt like she'd wasted a perfectly good day. She had considered emailing Aunty Ali to ask her permission to sell flowers from the cottage's gardens but had decided against it. She didn't want her precious idea tainted by her foul mood. Instead, she'd holed up in front of the television and sulked.

Now it was time for food and she couldn't really be bothered. She hauled herself out of the sofa, stomped through to the kitchen and went to the fridge, wishing something delicious would magically appear. Instead, there were all the fresh ingredients she'd piled into her trolley that morning... that she just didn't have the energy to do anything with.

She closed the fridge and turned to rummage in one

of the cupboards, pulling out a tube of Pringles. That would do.

Emmy went back through to the living room, grabbed the remote from the coffee table and settled back into her favourite corner of the old sofa.

Popping off the plastic lid and shoving a couple of crisps in her mouth, Emmy clicked through the channels until she found an old, black and white movie. Perfect. She settled back into the cushions and delved into the tube for another pile of crisps. She'd just managed to edge them out when her phone buzzed in her pocket, making her jump and scatter Pringles liberally all over herself and the sofa.

'Bollocks!' muttered Emmy, trying to gather them up without grinding any into the upholstery. Once half of them were safely back in the packet and the other half in her gob, she wiggled her phone out of her jeans pocket and unlocked the screen. A text. How old-school!

Hey Em. It's Jon. Sorry for being an arse earlier. I'm having a fire - would love it if you'd join me - we need to talk! Drinkies and cake on offer :) Please come. Jx

Emmy swallowed. What did he mean by "we need to talk"? Did he just want to apologise for being stroppy earlier? If so, wasn't his text apology enough?

She wasn't really feeling up to any kind of a scene. She just wanted to hide out in front of her film and pretend like the real world was on hold for a little while.

She glanced down at her phone and read the text again.

Please come.

Who was she kidding?! There was no way that she'd be able to settle to anything now, knowing that he was just over the lane, wondering if she'd turn up.

Making a snap decision, Emmy rushed up to the bathroom to wash off any stray Pringle crumbs and make sure that she at least looked vaguely human, then she grabbed a hoodie from her bedroom before running down to the kitchen. She quickly threw the rest of the Pringles and a pack of toffee popcorn into a carrier bag, before adding a bottle of pink wine. She didn't know what tonight was going to turn out like, but at least she'd have a bit of Dutch courage on hand if she needed it!

~

'You came!'

Jon grinned up at her from a camp chair. She'd spotted the flickering of the fire as soon as she'd entered the paddock, and had made her way over to his little patch of garden with a bunch of butterflies doing the conga in her chest.

'Of course!' she said, returning his smile uncertainly. Just the sight of him sent the conga line into overdrive.

'Take a pew. Can I get you a drink?'

'What are you having?' she asked, determined to take her cues from him, as she didn't really have a clue what was going on.

'Tea, fancy one?'

Emmy nodded.

'Two secs.' Jon bounded out of his chair and disappeared towards the door of the caravan.

Emmy carefully placed her bag of goodies down next to a second camp chair and went to stand in front of the fire that was blazing away in a handsome metal pit. It was like a giant scooped bowl which stood elevated by about a foot on an ornate stand.

'Here you go!'

She turned to find him holding out a tin camping mug for her.

'Perfect. Thanks,' she said, taking it carefully. Her fingers brushed his, and a zing of electricity seemed to shoot up her arm. She backed away quickly and sank into her chair, holding her cup in both hands, willing her heart rate to calm down a bit. What was it about this guy?

'Cheers,' said Jon, reaching his own mug across to her.

'Cheers,' she said, looking at him in surprise as she

chinked her tin mug against his with a resounding *thunk*.

'I'm so sorry about earlier,' he blurted. 'I had the hangover from hell. It was as much as I could do to stay upright long enough to answer the door.'

Emmy cast her mind back to the awkward encounter and a sudden snort of laughter escaped her, as all her nervous tension released in one blast. 'I thought you were really pissed off with me,' she chuckled.

Jon looked surprised. 'Pissed off? Nah! I was just trying not to completely embarrass myself. I... well, I didn't keep much breakfast down, let's put it like that,' he said delicately.

'Oh my...' Emmy paused as the laughter threatened to overtake her. 'And there I was, handing you beer and cake!'

Jon started laughing too. 'Things definitely got a bit dicey there. That's why I had to - shall we say - *cut our conversation short!*'

'I'm sorry,' said Emmy. 'I really didn't mean to make things worse!'

'How could you have known?!' said Jon, shaking his head. 'I'm really sorry you had to see me like that - that *anyone* had to see me like that!' he added ruefully.

'Happens to the best of us,' said Emmy, grinning at him as relief flooded through her. 'Oh jeez - is that what the bucket was for?!'

'Bucket?'

'I spotted one behind you-'

'Ah... well, if I'm honest, no. I mean, it did come in very handy after I'd shut the door in your face! But no. The van's roof leaks, so I keep a couple of buckets handy.'

Emmy's smile dropped. 'That sucks,' she said.

Jon shrugged and smiled at her. 'It's no big deal. Living in the caravan was never meant to be a permanent thing. It's done me proud just when I needed somewhere most, but I'm afraid the old girl is on her last legs.'

'Is that why you were meant to be moving into the cottage?' she asked, turning her gaze back to the fire, feeling awkward again.

'That was the idea - shelter away from the drips for a few months while I hunted for somewhere more permanent.'

'I'm sorry I messed that up for you,' she muttered, all the laughter disappearing in an instant.

'Em - like I said when you first arrived - it didn't really make much sense to move and then move again. I mean, I do love Dragonfly Cottage, but your need was way greater than mine.'

'But your place leaks!' she said miserably.

'But it's the spring!' He countered. 'I've just done a very long, wet winter in there - my second one, I'll have you know - and I survived. And I've got the spots for the buckets well sussed by this point.'

'But-'

'I mean it - drop it!' laughed Jon.

Emmy turned to him again and was relieved to see only friendly merriment on his face.

'Okay,' she sighed.

'Good,' he said. 'And for the record, I am *really* sorry about this morning. That was so sweet of you - and I was not exactly welcoming.'

'Don't worry about it,' said Emmy. 'I'm actually relieved it was just a hangover from hell and nothing I'd done. As we're doing the whole apology thing - that's why I came round earlier in the first place - to apologise.'

'What on earth for?' asked Jon, getting to his feet and adding a couple more logs to the fire.

'For snapping at you the day after I'd arrived. You were trying to be friendly and I bit your head off.'

'You did?' he said, the forced look of innocence on his face not quite hiding the fact that he remembered perfectly well.

Emmy nodded. 'You know I did. You said something about clearing my head and I overreacted.'

'Oh, that!' said Jon. 'That was no big deal. You were knackered and still hungover.'

'It was a bit more than that,' she said awkwardly. 'See, the thing is, my ex had a lovely habit of constantly having a go at me - subtle digs all the time - so I got into this horrible habit of jumping to conclusions, and assuming people mean the worst. I'm really sorry.'

'Your ex sounds like an asshat,' said Jon.

Emmy rolled her eyes and nodded her agreement.

'Anyway - you can forget about it. I'm just sorry you've been worrying about it all this time.'

'But I thought...' Emmy wasn't sure if she should ask - had she imagined the whole thing? No, she definitely hadn't. 'I thought that's why you've been so quiet? Something definitely changed after I had a go at you.' She paused and swallowed. 'You went all distant. Not that I blame you, of course!' she added.

'Em - has anyone ever told you that you worry too much?' asked Jon, shaking his head. 'I was just trying to give you a bit of space. You obviously weren't expecting me to be around the cottage as much as I have been - you *definitely* struggle with all the noise. I just wanted to give you the chance to settle in a bit - and I've tried to stay out of your hair. I didn't want you to feel like you had been thrown into some kind of weird house-share with me.'

Emmy was now staring at him, tin cup in hand. 'I'm such an idiot!' she breathed. 'Honestly, I've been so worried that I'd offended you. Then this morning, when I came to say I was sorry... and you were so off-'

'What a pair!' laughed Jon. 'Alright, enough of all that! Can we agree that we've both been idiots and just get on with being friends, please?'

Friends? Well, it was a start.

'Agreed!' said Emmy. 'Fancy a Pringle?' she added, realising that her appetite was back with a vengeance.

'Hungry?' he asked.

Emmy nodded. 'I didn't fancy anything much earlier.'

'Then I've got a better plan than crisps. Wait here a sec.'

Within a couple of minutes, he was back carrying a plate full of roughly sliced bread.

'Mmmm, bread!' said Emmy, raising her eyebrows, 'just what I fancied.'

'Hold your horses - it gets better,' Jon laughed, fishing around in his jacket pocket and drawing out a jar. 'Lucy's home-made raspberry jam!' he said with a flourish.

'Jam sandwiches?' said Emmy.

'My goodness you're impatient!' huffed Jon. He pulled out a pocket knife and disappeared again, this time in the direction of the hedge. Moments later he came back with a couple of long sticks, which he proceeded to sharpen into make-shift toasting forks.

'You're not serious?' said Emmy, as he handed one to her, then proceeded to stab a slice of bread with his own stick then holding it close to the flames.

'You've not lived until you've tried campfire toast with home-made jam,' he said seriously. 'Trust me.'

CHAPTER 14

Four slices of jam-smothered campfire toast later, Emmy finally put down her toasting stick and sat back with a contented sigh. Smokey, crispy, little burny bits. Mmmm!

'See, told you so,' said Jon with a grin.

'Alright smarty pants,' she laughed, 'you definitely win that one.'

'So, other than being growled at by me this morning, what have you been up to this weekend?' he asked curiously. 'You weren't in when I knocked last night before I went out.'

'Oh…' He'd knocked? He'd come to see her last night? Emmy gave herself a little mental shake and forced herself to answer the question. 'Erm, no. No, I wasn't. That bag you'd dropped in earlier was an invitation to a book club meeting with Caro and the girls.'

'So, you've been inducted into the mythical Little

Bamton book club already, have you? How very honoured you are!' he laughed.

'I'd hardly call it mythical - but it was a lot of fun.'

'I've never been to a book club. I always assumed it would be deadly dull.'

Emmy shook her head. 'Not this one. We spent all of three seconds talking about the book and then moved on to... other things,' she trailed off, realising with a blush that a high percentage of those *other things* had actually been to do with Jon himself.

She peeped over at him and caught him staring straight back at her.

'Do tell!' he said wiggling his eyebrows, clearly catching on to the fact that she was holding something back.

Emmy squirmed. Shit! What should she say? Flowers. Of course, fall back to the other half of her current obsession.

'Well... I had this idea that I wanted to run past them all. I'd like to set up a flower stall while I'm here,' she said, letting the words tumble out. Why did this feel scarier than telling the girls last night?

Jon raised his eyebrows. 'Not a bad plan!' he said.

'You think so?' she said, hating the fact that she sounded so unsure of herself.

'Well, don't you?' he laughed.

She nodded quickly. 'Scares me senseless, though,' she added honestly.

'All the best things should- at least a little bit, don't you think?'

'I guess...'

'Talk to me, Emmy. Give me the pros and cons.'

She pulled a face. Did he know what he was getting himself into here? 'Okay... cons,' she started.

'That's my girl - always the optimist starting with the positives first,' he laughed.

She picked up her toasting stick and prodded him with it - mainly to cover her delight at being called "my girl". Could she get any more desperate?

Jon swatted the stick away and winked at her.

'Okay then - pros,' she said, changing tack. 'It would be a way to earn a bit of money. I'd get some practise in - and get the chance to develop my own style away from Marjory.' She pulled a face and Jon laughed. 'Cons. I'd be raiding Ali's garden to do it - so basically selling flowers that aren't mine. I'm only due to be here in Little Bamton until she comes home - so if it worked I'd just be building things up only to have to stop again. Plus, if I wanted to grow anything of my own, I'd need to start sowing straight away, otherwise I'd be too late. And the flowers would only just be coming out in time for me to leave.'

'Right. You've thought about it quite a lot then?!' said Jon.

'Only non-stop,' she said with a rueful grin.

'Mind if I give you a few counter-arguments - just as a bit of outside perspective?'

'Please!' said Emmy. 'I feel like I've been circling the same loop.'

'Okay then - your cons list. Yes, you'd be using Ali's flowers - but she adores you. Email her. I bet you anything she'll be over the moon to be able to help. Now - your next con was being here for such a short time?'

Emmy nodded.

'Well, if you really want to move on when your aunt returns, you'll have had a chance to practice, like you said, build up a portfolio if you take some photos - and make some money while you're at it.

'It's not like you'd be committing to a lease on a shop. You could set something up really simply, have a great few weeks and then when it's time for you to go - no harm done and hopefully a lot of good.'

Emmy's heart squeezed, and it took her a moment to realise that what she was feeling wasn't excitement but a kind of wistful sadness. It already hurt to imagine moving away from the village - and it would be even worse if she built up this little business only to walk away from it.

'How does that sound?' prompted Jon.

'I just think it will be even harder to leave if I've put down roots like that.'

'Emmy - you know you don't *have* to leave the village when Ali comes back, don't you? You do have the option to stay.'

Emmy shook her head. 'I'm not sure Ali would be up for having a long-term house guest.'

'I don't necessarily mean with your aunt. You could look at finding somewhere here to rent if you wanted to.'

Emmy opened her mouth and closed it again. How come she hadn't even considered that as an option? Little Bamton had always equalled Dragonfly Cottage in her head - but Jon was right, it didn't have to be like that, did it? Thinking about it now both excited and scared the crap out of her in equal measures. She'd always just *ended up* in the places she lived before. This would be *choosing* to stay - something that carried quite a bit of weight because of her family history here.

'But if Ali was back in the cottage,' she said, 'I probably wouldn't be able to pick from her garden any more - meaning I wouldn't have any stock.'

'Maybe Ali would let you use a part of the paddock, or perhaps your new place might have a garden you could work with. If not, you could always look at renting a bit of land of your own.'

'Amber told me land around here is super-expensive at the moment,' countered Emmy.

Jon got up, threw another log on the fire and then turned to look at her. 'You're coming up with problems before they even happen!' he said, frustration evident in his voice.

Emmy watched as he drew in a deep breath and then took a couple of steps towards her. He stopped and reached out both his hands. Emmy hesitated for a moment before taking them. Jon pulled her to her feet so that she was looking him dead in the eye, her breath coming a little faster than was strictly necessary.

'You could go around in circles and keep finding reasons why this might not work - reasons it could fail before you even make a start,' he said in a tone that made the hairs on the back of Emmy's neck stand on end. He was still talking about the flower stall, right?! 'But you've got the option just to give it a try. Keep it simple and see if it works, then go from there. What have you got to lose?!'

Emmy gazed at him a moment, relishing the warmth of his hands wrapped around hers. If she didn't let go now, she was going to close the gap between them and kiss his face off.

Emmy gently dropped his hands and went to stare out across the rest of the paddock.

'You know,' she said, 'this morning I started to think about what I could do with a few extra beds out here,' she said, determined to sound more positive.

'That's a brilliant idea,' he said, coming to stand next to her again. 'Why not add that into your email to Ali? The worst she can say is no - and then at least you'd know what you've got to work with.'

Emmy nodded slowly. He was right. It was time to write that email.

'Thanks, Jon - you've really helped me think through everything,' she said.

'Good.' Jon leant over and nudged her shoulder gently with his. 'Just - don't keep thinking for too long, okay? Sometimes just getting on and doing rather than thinking is what's needed.'

'You might be right,' she said. Doing rather than thinking? If only she could apply that to how she felt about him as easily as she could to setting up the flower stall.

'I am, I promise!' he said, reaching his arm around her shoulders and giving her a friendly squeeze. 'And let me know if there's anything I can do to help, okay? Everything is way more simple than it looks.'

'Deal,' she said.

If only!

It had taken every ounce of resolve she had, but Emmy had bid Jon goodnight and headed back to the cottage just as dusk descended on the paddock. She'd used the excuse that she really wanted to go and send an email to her aunt before she chickened out. In reality, she didn't trust herself to sit next to Jon in the romantic firelight any longer without doing something about how she felt. And frankly, she could really do without that added complication so soon after they'd made up!

She couldn't believe that it had only been a matter of weeks since Chris had walked out on her. Back in Bristol, she'd sworn off men and thought it would be months, if not years before she would be even remotely interested in another relationship. But there was something about Jon that drew her in - he'd gotten well and truly under her skin.

Emmy quickly made herself a cup of tea and took it through to the conservatory. While she waited for her laptop to fire up, she brutally forced all thoughts of Jon to the back of her mind. She needed to get this email just right.

In a way, she would have preferred to talk Ali through her ideas - but she wasn't sure what her aunt's itinerary was, and didn't want to put her on the spot. So she loaded her email with all her ideas for the stall, raiding the gardens for the flowers, and asked about the possibility of creating a couple of extra cut-flower beds in the paddock.

As soon as she hit send, Emmy sat back in her chair and raised both fists above her head in a little victory dance. She'd done it. She'd taken the first steps and it was out of her hands until she heard back.

Now, she desperately needed to tell someone about this exciting step in proceedings! She briefly considered going back over to see Jon, but quickly vetoed the idea. Too dangerous. Too complicated. She picked up her mobile and went to dial her mum's number, but paused. She wasn't ready to tell her mum about everything yet… she didn't want to jinx things. Crap, if she didn't tell someone she was going to go mad!

If only it was Saturday night and she could see the book club girls. Of course - she would call Caro!

'I've done it!' squealed Emmy down the phone as soon as Caro picked up.

'Hi Emmy!' laughed Caro. 'You sound a bit brighter than this morning.'

'Oh, yeah - sorry about that. I had a lot on my mind.'

'I noticed. And... you've done *what* exactly?' She asked curiously.

'Phase one of the Little Bamton Flower Stall Project has been initiated.'

CHAPTER 15

Emmy woke to the sound of birdsong the next morning and found herself grinning like an idiot into her pillow. There was a huge bubble of happiness in her chest - it had been so long since she'd felt like this that it took her a moment or two to recognise the sensation.

She could hear Jon moving about downstairs, already hard at work at whatever was on today's list of jobs… she'd rather lost track. One thing she did know, however, was that if he was in the cottage, it must be after nine. Oops - another unintentional lie-in! Today was the day she was going to get everything ready to launch the flower stall. She wanted to be ready for the off as soon as she heard back from Aunty Ali. Even if her aunt didn't agree to her plans, Emmy was determined to find another way to make this dream work.

Just the thought of it made Emmy hug herself with

joy again. She and Caro had talked for nearly an hour the previous night as Emmy filled her in on how much Jon's advice had mirrored their own at book club, and what exactly she'd asked Ali for.

'This sounds like you might be planning on staying in the village a bit longer then…' Caro had said excitedly when Emmy told her about her ideas for the paddock. Emmy's answer to that had simply been "watch this space".

Much to her surprise, Caro hadn't given her the third degree about Jon. On one hand, she'd been grateful for her restraint but on the other, she'd longed to go all swoony about him and tell Caro just how rampant her daydreams about him had become.

Emmy wriggled, then threw the duvet back. It wouldn't do to let her mind wander down that particular path when Jon was just downstairs!

She quickly grabbed her phone and powered it up. She'd turned it off the night before to stop herself from checking her notifications every ten minutes. She wasn't particularly hot on the time difference between England and Aus, but she was pretty sure that she was most likely to receive a reply during the night. Even so, she hardly dared to hope that she'd get one this quickly.

The usual flurry of notifications pinged in, and Emmy hastily flicked through to her emails.

There was a reply. Bless her lovely, lovely aunt! She

wasn't going to have to waste days climbing the walls after all.

Dear Emmy,

How lovely to hear from you. I'm having a wonderful time here thanks - though the days are disappearing on me rather too quickly!

I'm glad you're enjoying your stay in Dragonfly Cottage so much. I LOVE your idea - it's just what the village needs, and I think it will be really successful. Does this mean you might be planning to stay in Little Bamton longer than just the three months?

Of course you are more than welcome to help yourself to any flowers from the walled garden - and the front garden too - though it would be nice if you didn't completely empty the front so that it still looks pretty! All I'd ask is that you go easy on the shrubs. A little light trimming is fine of course, but if you need larger amounts of greenery, have a look at what you can cut over in the paddock, there are all sorts of shrubby bits over near the river.

Speaking of the paddock - yes, you're welcome to set up some growing beds over there - as long as you check it's okay with Jon first. I'd suggest you seek out Alf for some advice before making a start - he has a lot to do with the allotments and the girls in the pub should be able to introduce you. He'll be able to advise on how to set them up to get the most out of them. You'd better get a wiggle on though, otherwise you're going to be starting late. Oh, and Alf's a good source of well-rotted horse manure too!

All I'd ask is that you avoid anything permanent - so no long-term planting and the beds should be movable. Soil and compost can easily be raked out and re-seeded, so don't worry about that - but no concrete pathways or similar! Just make sure that the space can be returned to near enough its original state and you won't go far wrong.

Emmy - I'm so excited! Make sure you take lots of pics and send me them as you go.

I have to run - we're off out for a meal. Send me updates soon,

love, Aunty Ali xxx

P.S. I have a seed-buying addiction. Please help yourself to anything you fancy from my tins. They're in the conservatory in the little chest of drawers next to the sofa. They need using up so I can buy more next winter ;)

Emmy read the whole email at speed and then went back to the beginning again and read it more slowly. Then she let out an excited squeal, tumbled off the bed and jumped up and down like a three-year-old on a bouncy castle. Her aunt had said yes - to everything!

The excited bubble she'd woken up with had now grown so huge, she didn't feel like she could contain it.

'Emmy?!' There was an urgent knock at the door, then Jon burst into the room. 'You okay? I heard you scream!'

Emmy, who had whirled around to face him, started to giggle.

'Oh my god, what?!' laughed Jon, looking her up and down, clearly trying to work out if she'd completely lost the plot. Given that she was standing there in her thread-bare PJs, phone still clutched in one hand and a totally manic grin on her face, he might have a point.

'She said yes!' gasped Emmy.

'What? Who?' said Jon, a frown on his face as he desperately tried to catch up.

'Ali!' said Emmy. 'Aunty Ali said yes - I can have all the flowers I want for the stall, and I can put beds up in the paddock - as long as it's okay with you - and she said I can raid her seed stash too!' she finished in a rush.

'Of course she did!' laughed Jon. 'Ali is amazing. I *told* you!!' he was beaming at her now.

'Thank you for everything!' said Emmy, taking a couple of steps towards him.

Jon shook his head. 'This is all you, Em - you just needed a sounding post. So, when are you going to start?'

'Tomorrow,' she said with a little squeak.

'I'm so excited for you,' he said. 'Come here!'

Jon took Emmy completely by surprise by closing the distance between them and gathering her up into a warm hug.

She squeezed him back, breathing in the scent of

him. Then she remembered that there was nothing other than a thin layer of worn flannel between her modesty and the guy she was already struggling to contain herself around.

She gently disentangled herself from the hug and grinned sheepishly at him.

'Thanks,' she said, a weird wave of shyness washing over her.

'Coffee?' asked Jon, retreating a couple of steps towards the door, looking a bit pink in the cheeks.

Emmy nodded. 'I'll be down in just a sec.'

As soon as he disappeared, Emmy slumped down onto the edge of her bed to text Caro and let her know that Ali had agreed to her plans. She hit send and hugged her phone to her for a second. She could barely believe how much her life had changed in the last few weeks, and how much it was likely to change again. The one thing she knew for certain was that there was no way she'd want to go back to how it was before. She had to make this work!

With that, she bounced up off the bed and started to throw her clothes on. She had so much to do, there was no time to lose.

The night was closing in fast, but Emmy was completely cosy and content, working away to set her newly-cut flowers to condition overnight. The conservatory felt like a comforting, flower-filled oasis as darkness fell on the garden outside.

From the moment she'd put down her empty coffee cup and followed Jon over to his caravan to fetch the trestle table he'd offered to lend her, the day had been a whirlwind.

Caro had offered to accompany her into town to buy all the little bits and pieces she needed to make a start on things. She'd explained that she had to keep her spending as low as possible - but that hadn't stopped her from stocking up on a few special bits and pieces to make the stall look its very best for its debut outing.

Caro had poo-pooed the idea of going to the expensive hardware store first and had instead insisted that they raid the pound shop. Emmy was thrilled with their spoils. She'd managed to buy a set of large plastic buckets for cutting and conditioning the flowers. Then there was a massive roll of thick, brown paper and some natural garden twine for presenting everything. At the last minute, she'd added a pack of ten little slate hearts to her trolley - she figured she could use them to write her prices on in chalk marker.

She hadn't found anything she was happy with for displaying the flowers on the table though. She was just starting to panic when Caro suggested they take a walk down to the tip and recycling centre "just in case".

Caro's hunch had proved an absolute life-saver, and they'd discovered a stash of ten galvanised buckets - all different shapes and sizes and some a little dented in places - but she'd agreed with Caro when she declared that it "only added to their charm."

Emmy looked at them now, lined up along the opposite wall, ready to receive her newly wrapped and arranged offerings in the morning.

When they'd got back to Little Bamton, she'd taken the trestle table down to the corner and set it up, ready for her early-morning visit. She was planning to make several trips with the buckets, and carry them all down by hand rather than load them in the back of the car.

Then, she'd spent the rest of the afternoon, champing at the bit, desperate to get started on cutting the flowers for the morning. She made a meticulous list of exactly what she needed and what she was planning to sell, but she knew the magic would only kick in when she actually made a start. And then, finally, the time had come, and she'd ventured out into the cool evening garden to cut flowers for her stall for the very first time.

Emmy sighed, straightened up from the final bucket and looked around her. Now all she had to do was to stop herself from reciting her to-do list. Cut flowers - done. Condition flowers - on it. Sleep - highly unlikely. Then tomorrow - get up early, arrange and wrap flowers, arrange the table… then what? Sit back and wait for the customers to turn up, she guessed.

Emmy's stomach lurched with nerves. She knew she was being silly. This plan had barely cost her anything to set up, and its success wasn't based on one day. But still, she needed it to work. Something deep in her heart needed it to work.

She turned to her buckets of flowers one more time, drinking in the beautiful colours, and let out a long, low breath. She was ready.

CHAPTER 16

Seven am already. Emmy yawned. She hadn't been up at this time of day for a very long time, let alone having already completed an hour and a half's work by this point. She knew that she didn't really need to have the stall set up so early, but something about it felt right - and she'd decided to follow her gut instinct. She wanted her flowers to be ready to greet even the earliest risers.

She picked up the last two buckets and carried them through from the conservatory to the front garden. She could, of course, have popped them all in the back of her car and driven them down the lane in one go - but she'd decided to relay them all to the front gate and then carry them down instead. After all, it wasn't far, and she somehow didn't want to spoil the peace of such a beautiful morning with the roar of her engine.

Emmy headed out onto the lane with the first two

buckets in hand and glanced briefly across the paddock, its grass silvery with the heavy dew. Her eyes caught a hint of Jon's caravan through a gap in the hedge, and her stomach gave an unexpected lurch at the thought of him, no more than a few meters away, fast asleep. She wondered if he slept naked?

What? Wah! What was she thinking?! Emmy gave herself a little shake and strode quickly down the lane towards the corner where her table was ready and waiting. She could feel her cheeks burning bright in the cold morning air. She needed to focus on the task in hand, not whether certain insanely hot men slept in the nuddy!

Right.

Table.

Flowers.

Emmy popped the two heavy buckets onto the surface and sighed. She hoped she'd prepared enough. The temptation to go absolutely mad and fill the entire table with beautiful bouquets had been huge, but as she'd set about cutting what she needed the previous day, she'd decided to start with a smaller selection. After all, very few people knew about her little venture yet and there would be nothing worse than having to bring every single flower back home at the end of the day.

So, she'd filled six of her ten buckets. Even with this small amount, she was well aware that Dragonfly Cottage might still end up filled with unsold flowers by that evening. It didn't really matter. The important thing was that she was actually doing this - and she hadn't felt this happy for a very long time.

Two trips later, she was slightly regretting the decision to ferry the flowers by hand rather than by car. But as she lifted the final, fragrant bucket onto the table, she felt an overwhelming sense of accomplishment.

She quickly shuffled the buckets around so that they looked their best and then took out her phone and snapped a couple of shots to email to Aunty Ali. It looked a little sparse, and she longed for the day when she could fill the whole table and the ground in front of it, knowing that every single stem would sell. But - it was a start.

The bunches of daffodils seemed to glow inside their brown paper wrappers in the morning light. Emmy thought they looked gorgeous all standing together in their two galvanised buckets. She drew the stack of little slate hearts out of the cloth tote-bag over her shoulder, searched for the one with the corresponding price, and gently placed it in front of them.

Next was a couple of smaller buckets, one filled with beautifully scented hyacinths and the other bursting with bunches of early tulips. She'd decided to sell the tulips in bouquets of individual colours - her favourites were a gorgeous, soft apricot, but there was definitely something to be said for the bold pink variety she'd pilfered from the front garden too.

The final two buckets were the ones that had taken Emmy the most time to prepare. These held her carefully hand-tied creations. No two were the same, but each one was like a miniature-cottage-garden in its own right. Bursting with fragrance and colour and bound together by the fresh greens that only spring could provide. These were more expensive and were a bit of an experiment to see if there was any interest in them. Emmy had everything crossed that there was, as these were the flowers that she'd put her heart and soul into.

Emmy was just starting to wander back up to Dragonfly Cottage in search of some breakfast when she paused, let out a laugh and turned back to the table. She'd forgotten one last - but rather important - detail. She reached her hand into her bag again and pulled out an old tin piggy bank in the shape of a milk churn. She'd found it at the tip on the "donations" shelf, and had picked it up for fifty pence. She placed it carefully in front of the buckets, with a small prayer that it would be safe. She knew that she'd have to come up with something a little bit more secure at some point - but for now, this was perfect.

∼

The waft of frying bacon that washed over Emmy as she let herself back into the cottage made her stomach growl.

'Hello?!' she called, kicking her shoes off in the hallway and padding through to the kitchen.

'Surprise!' Jon grinned at her from over by the hob, holding the handle of the heavy cast-iron frying pan with one hand and wielding a spatula with the other.

'It certainly is!' laughed Emmy. 'How on earth did you sneak in here without me seeing you?'

'I waited till I saw you picking up the second batch of buckets and hot-footed it over here while you had your back turned,' he grinned. 'I thought your first day in business deserved a little celebration.'

Emmy shook her head. 'Thank you,' she said. She couldn't stop grinning.

'My pleasure. Now - how do you like your eggs?'

It was only a matter of minutes before she was sitting in front of a plate full-to-bursting with the most delicious fry-up. Eggs - perfectly golden and runny in the middle, bacon, sausages, toast, beans, mushrooms and even black pudding.

'Hope you're hungry!' Jon grinned, as he placed a freshly-brewed mug of coffee down next to her plate.

'Wow! Thanks,' said Emmy, her stomach giving another ravenous growl in answer. 'Erm - please tell me you're having some too?' she demanded.

'You didn't think I was going to miss out, did you?' he laughed, quickly collecting a second plate and his own cup of coffee. 'Tuck in - you've been up since sparrow-fart! I'm guessing the stall is all set up and ready for its first customers?'

Emmy nodded as she shook a wave of tomato ketchup onto her plate, dipped a sausage into it and bit it in half. Chewing rapidly, she drew her phone out of her pocket, clicked through to the photos she'd taken for Ali, and passed it across the table to Jon.

'Wow, it looks great!' he said admiringly.

'It looked a little bit empty - but I didn't want to have to bring too many flowers home tonight if they don't sell,' she said, slathering butter on a slice of toast.

'You don't need to have everything spot-on straight away. I'm guessing you'll learn loads by a bit of trial and error.'

'Yup! And it feels amazing to have made a start! Thank you so much for doing this,' she said, happily forking up mushrooms. 'It's made it feel like a real occasion.'

'My pleasure. And anyway, that's just the way it should feel. I think we need a toast!' said Jon, putting down his knife and fork and picking up his mug of coffee.

Emmy grabbed hers too.

'Here's to… wait, have you got a name for it?'

'For what?' she giggled.

'Your stall. Your business!' he said.'

It took a matter of seconds for a name to pop into her head. 'What do you think of "Grandad Jim's"?' she asked.

'Spot on!' he said, smiling approvingly. 'Here's to Grandad Jim's being a huge success.'

Emmy grinned at him as she chinked her mug lightly against his.

'So, what's next? I guess you're done with the stall until this evening?' said Jon, before stuffing almost an entire fried egg in his mouth in one go, making Emmy laugh.

'Well - I want to raid Aunty Ali's seed stash to see what she's got that I might be able to get on and sow for the new beds. I'll only go for annuals - some of them come up fast enough that I might just be able to start cutting them before I have to move on.'

Jon nodded, his face suddenly serious. 'No plans to stay when Ali comes back?'

Emmy shrugged. 'Like I said to Caro - watch this space. I love Little Bamton. If the stall does well… it's another reason to stay.'

Jon mopped up the last of his egg with a piece of toast, then put his knife and fork down with a sigh, and picked up his coffee again.

'Em… I was wondering…'

Emmy looked up quickly from her plate. Jon's face was unusually serious. She raised her eyebrows questioningly.

'Well - have you ever been to Bamton Hall?'

Whatever she'd been expecting him to ask, it hadn't been that. She shook her head. 'No! I've always wanted to though. Nan and Grandad Jim used to go on romantic walks around the gardens quite a lot. I think that's why they never took me there - it was their place, you know? Why'd you ask?'

'They've got their first plant sale up there on Saturday morning - and... I wondered if you fancied going?' he paused and cleared his throat. 'Erm, with me,' he added as if she might not have picked up on that bit.

'Ooh, yes please. I'd love to!' said Emmy with a grin. Plants and the chance to spend some time getting to know Jon? Could this day get any better?

'Great!' he said, returning her grin. 'I'm doing a bit of work on the house next week, so I want to drop a few things off from the van while we're there.'

Emmy nodded, now a little unsure whether this was a date, or whether she'd just been invited along for the ride. She quickly decided that she was more than happy either way!

'Just make sure you bring plenty of fifty pence pieces. According to Sue, who suggested it when I bumped into her the other day, the old dears sell everything ridiculously cheaply, but never have enough change.'

'Roger that!' said Emmy. 'I wonder if any of them will have some trays of seedlings to buy. It would be great if I could get a bit of a head start. I'm a bit late for a first sowing now that we're into April.

'If they're anything like Ali - I'd say it's pretty definite there will be something. She was always giving spares away. I think that's her favourite part of gardening you know, growing the seedlings.'

Emmy laughed. 'Yeah - she mentioned she was a seed-addict.'

⁓

They were just finishing off the washing up between them when someone hammered at the door. Emmy glanced at the clock and was surprised to see that they'd managed to gossip away half the morning over the delicious celebratory breakfast.

'You expecting any deliveries today?' she asked, half assuming that it would be yet another essential bit of kit arriving.

Jon shook his head. 'Nope - must be for you.'

Emmy dried her hands and headed out to the front door.

'Hey Emmy!'

Amber and Caro were at the door, grinning at her like loons.

'Hi! What brings you two here?'

'Your stall,' said Caro.

'What's happened? Is there a problem?' she said quickly.

'Oh no, nothing like that,' said Amber quickly.

'You've already sold out, Emmy!' squealed Caro.

'Very funny,' said Emmy, rolling her eyes.

'She's being serious!' said Amber. 'We came down

for our own flowers earlier, then we bumped into Sue. She saw my tulips and wanted the same ones - those apricot coloured ones - but she couldn't come over because had someone turning up at her place for an appointment. So I gave her mine and came back to get another bunch… and they've all gone.'

Amber finally paused for breath.

'What's happening?' asked Jon appearing behind her.

'I've sold out of tulips,' said Emmy.

'No, Emmy - you've sold out of everything,' said Caro with a giggle, as she realised that it wasn't sinking in.

'Everything,' repeated Amber. 'We came to bring you this,' said Amber, thrusting a very heavy milk-churn money box at her.

Emmy promptly burst into tears.

CHAPTER 17

As they trundled along the narrow country lane in his van, Emmy stole a glance at Jon. She'd never seen him looking so... tidy! Smart, dark jeans, a navy shirt over a soft grey tee shirt - and a pair of new-ish looking tan boots rather than the tatty, splattered work pair she was used to him wearing. It made her feel pretty scruffy in comparison.

Emmy had been up super-early. She kept telling herself it was because she wanted to get the stall all stocked up and ready to roll for the day, and still leave her enough time to get ready to head out with Jon. In reality, she woke super-early because she was a ball of nervous excitement.

It didn't help that she wasn't really sure if this was just an outing between friends... or whether it was actually a date.

The moment he knocked on the door rather than

let himself in as usual, Emmy knew that they were on untested ground.

She looked down at herself. Man, she really should have made more of an effort. She was wearing her favourite pink cord dungarees, yellow welly-boots, and she'd bundled her hair back out of the way under a matching mustard-yellow bobble-hat that she'd spotted in Caro's shop and hadn't been able to resist.

Ah well, hadn't she promised herself that she was never going to pretend to be anything other than exactly who she was from now on? Well, this was who she was - pink dungarees and all.

'Nearly there,' said Jon.

'Great!' she replied.

It had been like this ever since they got in the van - strangely stilted and formal.

'Thanks again for asking me to come,' she said, instantly curling her fingers into a fist until her nails dug into her palms. She sounded like such a plonker.

'My pleasure,' he replied. Then let out a little huff of air.

'You okay?' she asked instinctively.

'Honestly?'

'Of course!'

'I'm nervous,' he said, then cleared his throat awkwardly.

'Oh.' She didn't really know what to say. 'Me too.'

'You are?'

Emmy nodded.

'Huh.

Emmy snorted.

'What?' he demanded, sounding a lot more like his usual self.

'What a pair,' Emmy giggled. 'I've just been sitting here worrying about what I'm wearing.'

'You look fab - as always,' he said bluntly.

Emmy coloured. 'Well, for the record, so do you.'

'Thanks. Right, that's enough of this silliness. Agreed?'

'Yup!' She grinned at him and he briefly reached over and squeezed her hand.

'It's down here,' he said, letting go and indicating to turn between two grand stone pillars.

Emmy's jaw dropped as they trundled down a long driveway and a stunning mansion-house appeared in front of them.

'Jeez - it's got turrets,' she said.

Jon chuckled, drew his van onto a gravelled parking spot in front of the house and killed the engine. For a moment, they just sat and stared.

'Right,' she said, breaking the silence that was just starting to feel a little awkward again. 'Take me to the plants or lose me forever.'

∼

Emmy stared in horror at the garden bench where she'd gathered her spoils. It was practically groaning under the weight of trays and pots that she simply hadn't been able to leave behind.

Jon had walked with her around to the back lawn where the plant sale was taking place but had quickly left her to meander at her own sweet will while he went to unload the van.

They'd agreed to meet back here when they were both finished. Emmy was dreading the look on his face when he spotted her mountain of spoils. She wasn't even sure they'd fit into the van.

She'd quickly come to realise that she was a little bit too early for there to be many annual seedlings up for grabs, but she had managed to score six trays of cornflowers that one gent had autumn-sown and then overwintered. She couldn't wait until the sturdy little plants started to flower. There be a mix of blues, pinks, whites and even a purple that was so dark it was almost black.

Another stall had individual wallflower plants available in two-litre pots. These already had some flower buds on them, and they looked like they'd be ready to start flowering really soon. She was pretty sure that this was far from the most efficient and cost-effective way to fill her flower beds, but frankly, she didn't care. These were going for a song, and she had the takings from the stall to play with!

Emmy had bought two dozen plants - half dark red, half bright orange - from the delighted woman. They'd both look and smell amazing dotted into her bouquets, and she'd have plenty of space to pop them out in the paddock as soon as she had the beds ready. For now, they'd have to be okay in their pots.

Sal, the lady who was managing the stall, took an interest in what she was up to, and so Emmy explained all about *Grandad Jim's Flowers*. Sal promised to visit next time she was passing, then pointed her in the direction of several of the other stalls.

Emmy ended up with several trays of sweet pea seedlings, a large chunk of Crocosmia that one man was giving away because it was taking over his garden, and three gigantic pots of Siberian iris clumps. They'd take an epic hole to sink them into, but Emmy couldn't wait to add their rich purple-and-yellow blooms to the stall.

'Okay - remind me never to leave you unattended near plants for sale ever again!' laughed Jon as he appeared next to her.

'I know, I know - I'm sorry,' said Emmy, yanking her hat off and running her fingers through her hair. 'I got a bit carried away.'

Jon shook his head, but he was grinning at her.

'They're going to be amazing though - I couldn't leave them behind!'

'I'll let you off the hook!' he chuckled. 'Shall we get this lot to the van, then find a cuppa?'

It took an age for them to haul all the plants from the back lawn around to the van. Even worse, no matter how carefully Jon tried to fit them all in, there just wasn't room for them all as well as his tools in the back.

'Okay - I've got a plan. I'll stash some of my gear here until I come back next week. I'm sure Horace won't mind, and I don't need them until the job here anyway.

'Are you sure?' she asked, her cheeks glowing- both with the effort of carrying the heavy pots, and the mild mortification she was currently succumbing to.

'Of course. Can't leave your plant-babies behind, can we?' he deadpanned.

She smirked at him and shook her head decidedly. 'Thanks, Jon.'

'My pleasure,' he replied, echoing his words from earlier, but minus the uncomfortable undercurrent. 'Come here a sec,' he said, reaching out and tugging on both her dungaree straps to draw her close. 'You've got dirt on your face.'

He gently ran his index finger down the bridge of her nose.

Emmy's breath caught in her throat and her eyes locked on his as she tilted her face to stare at him. He had a little half-smile on his face. She couldn't look away as he traced his fingertips over her cheekbone and tucked a strand of hair behind her ear.

Emmy shivered, desperately wanting to reach out and touch him, but not wanting to break the spell that seemed to have fallen over them.

'Emmy, I-'

She never found out what he was about to say, as, unable to stop herself, she raised herself onto her tiptoes and planted a soft kiss on his lips.

Jon seemed to freeze for just a moment before winding his fingers into her hair and kissing her back.

It was several long seconds before they broke apart.

'So… the plants…' said Jon, looking slightly dazed.

'Right…' she said.

Jon grinned, wrapping an arm around her and drawing her back towards him again. 'They'll wait.'

~

Darkness had fallen early. The skies over Little Bamton had been growing grumpier all afternoon and the leaden clouds that had haunted the village promised a serious amount of rain. But Emmy didn't mind. She was too busy reliving the hour she and Jon had spent wandering through Bamton Hall's gardens, diving into secluded spots to steal a kiss, only to emerge giggling like a pair of teenagers.

Things had turned a little more guarded when they climbed out of his van back in Little Bamton. He'd helped her to unload her goodies into the front garden and then had headed back to his caravan. Half of her was gutted that he hadn't come in for a cuppa, but the other half was secretly glad for the chance to let everything sink in a bit.

Her and Jon. It really had happened, hadn't it?

She brought her fingers up to her lips, her mind reliving that first kiss. Yep - those kisses had *definitely* happened. Her lips still felt all tingly and plump.

Emmy hugged herself and headed out into the conservatory. She'd decided against stocking the flower stall on Sundays, so there was no prep to do this evening. She felt a little bit lost without the jobs that had already become a part of her routine. Plus she was having a hard time taking her mind off the gorgeous man just across the lane. She needed a distraction.

Seeds. She'd raid Aunty Ali's seed stash. The conservatory held everything she needed to get sowing, and she was already pretty late in the season to make a start on it.

Emmy went over to the chest of drawers where Ali had said her seed tins were stashed, drew them out and sat down with them on the sofa. She popped the lids off and gasped.

Ali really hadn't been kidding when she'd said that she was addicted to buying from the seeds catalogues! She rifled through the packets, excitement blooming in her chest. To start with, there were half a dozen varieties of sweet-peas, along with a whole bunch of annuals that Emmy was desperate to grow. Zinnias, Cornflowers, Cosmos, Ammi, Larkspur… the list went on. Bless her lovely, lovely aunt - this was going to save her a fortune!

She'd have the new beds out in the paddock built, filled and nicely settled in time to plant these babies out as soon as they were ready. Sure, they might flower a bit late, but...

Emmy's heart gave a little twang as she realised that she might have already left Dragonfly Cottage by the time some of these flowered. Whether she'd also have left the village by then remained to be seen. She gave herself a quick shake. There was no point worrying about that yet, and in any case, the worst-case scenario was that she could fill the cottage's two gardens with all this beauty for Aunty Ali to enjoy instead.

A rumble outside forced Emmy off the sofa. She went to the double doors and stared out into the dark garden just as the skies opened. It was like someone had turned the tap on out there.

Emmy didn't mind. She loved storms. She was just about to throw one of the doors open when she thought of Jon, over in the caravan. The *leaking* caravan. Oh *hell* no. There was no way she was going to leave him out there to get soaked.

Emmy dashed through the cottage, thrust her feet into her wellies and grabbed one of her aunt's old waterproof jackets from the hooks in the hallway. Throwing it hastily over her shoulders, she did up the zip and stepped out into the downpour.

Shit shit shit! This rain was incredibly... wet! She set off at a trot down the garden path, but by the time she'd scaled the paddock gate and jumped down the other side, she could already feel water making its way through the seams of the coat. The hood refused to stay up as she ran, and rivulets of water spiralled down her hair and under her collar.

She skidded to a halt at the caravan door and thumped on it. Two seconds later, Jon answered with a half-anxious, half-amused expression on his face.

'Emmy! Is everything alright?' he said, reaching out and pulling her out of the rain.

The inside of the caravan was blissfully cosy and warm after her drenching, and as Emmy stood there, dripping onto the doormat, she suddenly felt foolish.

'I… erm, I didn't want you to get wet,' she mumbled.

'So you decided to swim over here and…'

'I thought you might like to come over to the cottage,' she said, going pink in the face, and wriggling as a drip made its way down her spine.

'What, go out in that?' he laughed, 'you must be mad!'

'Seems so,' she said, watching as a single drip plopped leisurely down from the caravan's ceiling into a bucket. He was hardly having to bail himself out over here. 'Okay. I'd better go.'

'Wait a sec!' said Jon with a laugh, grabbing her hand. 'Take a leaf out of Charlie's book!'

'Eh?' she said, looking around, confused. She was starting to shiver now, the cold, wet cotton of her tee-shirt clinging to her.

Jon pointed over to the foot of his bed, where Charlie was stretched out, fast asleep.

'First things first,' said Jon, drawing her towards

him. He unzipped her jacket and chucked it unceremoniously onto the floor near the door. Emmy shivered again, but this time because Jon was kissing her cheek. Then her neck.

Then he grabbed a towel from the bed behind him, plonked it right over her head and began to rub her hair so vigorously that she started to giggle.

CHAPTER 18

Surely this was the only way to wake up on a Sunday morning? Emmy snuggled deeper into the arms that were around her and sighed.

Wait, arms? She peeped around her, taking in the low ceiling, buckets in the middle of the floor and birdsong that felt like it was just feet away. A grin spread across her face. Of course, she was in the caravan. And these were Jon's arms.

Emmy curled her toes in happiness. This hadn't been her plan when she'd made her mad dash across the paddock in the pouring rain - but plans be damned!

Once she got warm and dry and was wearing one of his huge, warm jumpers like a mini-dress, they'd shared a beer and then spent the night behaving like a pair of naughty teenagers.

It was only when a disgruntled Charlie had yowled to be let out at about two in the morning that Emmy noticed it had stopped raining. Her suggestion that she should probably head back to the cottage too had been met by Jon returning to the bed and wrapping her in the duvet to prevent her escape. His kiss had put the idea of leaving firmly out of her mind.

Emmy felt her cheeks flush and she wriggled again.

'Morning Em.' Jon's voice was thick with sleep, and she smiled as he tightened his arms around her. Shouldn't this feel awkward? Uncomfortable? Scary? All Emmy felt right now was incredibly cosy and happy.

'Morning,' she sighed. 'I guess I should head over and give Charlie his breakfast in a bit.'

In response, Jon drew her even closer and kissed the back of her neck, making her squirm.

'Not till you've had coffee. And breakfast,' he said.

'Twisted my arm!' she turned and smiled at him.

How? How could anyone possibly look that sexy after just a few hours sleep squished into a tiny little bed? She dreaded to think what she looked like right now - she could only imagine her hair was a fright-wig after the vigorous towelling he'd given it the night before. Ah well, who cared? She flopped back down onto the pillow and yawned widely.

'Oh no you don't, no going back to sleep missy!' chuckled Jon, climbing over her and heading into the little galley kitchen. 'Time to fill you full of coffee, I think!'

'It's Sunday,' groaned Emmy, 'what's the rush?'

'Well, no rush really, only Sam called me yesterday afternoon to tell me he had some wood for you. *Something* must have made me forget to tell you,' he said with a wink.

'Sam...?' Emmy was wracking her brains. She knew the name...

'Caro's other half!' chuckled Jon. 'Seriously Em, you're so wrapped up with your flowers I think you're away with the fairies half the time.'

Emmy grinned at him. Just a couple of weeks ago and this comment would have made her hit the roof and turn as prickly as a balled-up ball of prickly things - but now it just made her laugh and shrug - because he was right, and it didn't seem to bother him anyway.

'So Sam's got wood?' she prompted.

Jon smirked at the innuendo. 'Exciting hey? He's going to drop it down later. We'll be able to make a start on your new beds - that's if you fancy a hand?'

'That would be great!' she said, excitement in her voice. 'I was just going through Ali's seeds last night when...'

'When you decided to swim over and rescue me?'

'Yeah - that! Ooh, thanks,' she said, gratefully taking a tin mug of coffee from him and shifting over so that he could sit next to her, their backs resting against the bank of pillows.

She took a sip, and let out a sigh of pleasure.

'Steady on there, unless you want to be held hostage in bed for the rest of the day!'

Emmy snorted.

'A -ny-waaayy…' he drawled, flushing slightly, 'any of the seeds useful?'

Emmy nodded enthusiastically. 'Basically all of them - and I probably won't need to buy any others. Aunty Ali really is a compulsive seed buyer. I'm a bit late to get planting, but I should be able to get some to flower before my three months is up.'

Jon nodded, his face suddenly serious.

'It made me a bit sad, you know,' she said, 'I love being here, and Dragonfly is so full of amazing memories, I hate the thought of leaving it.'

'I can imagine,' said Jon quietly.

Emmy nodded. 'Hey - I remember you saying you moved around a lot when you were a kid, but where's your family settled now?'

Jon took a slow sip of his coffee, then cradled his mug between his hands. 'I don't really have any family,' he said. 'I never knew my dad. Mum was really young when she had me. She tried, but… well, I spent quite a bit of time with my Grandma when I was little. She died when I was five. Mum couldn't cope. I ended up in foster care, and that's where I stayed. Then mum died when I was seven. An overdose.'

'I'm so sorry,' breathed Emmy.

Jon shook his head. 'It was a very, very long time ago. I had some great foster families along the way - some, not quite so great - but none of them ever stuck for very long. I got used to looking after myself.'

He went quiet for a moment, and Emmy leaned her head on his shoulder. 'What brought you to Little Bamton?' she asked eventually.

'Work!' he said. 'I was living in this shitty little bedsit in Exeter, doing handy-man work for the university to save up for a better place and to be able to take my Gas Safe exams. Then I heard on the grapevine that Bamton Hall needed some old plumbing re-doing as an emergency. The guy they'd booked to do it had put his back out. I got in touch with Horace, the owner, and said I was available as long as I could do the work in the evenings and at weekends so that it could fit in around my job. He was so over the moon to find someone, I don't think he'd have minded if I'd asked to work right through the night!'

'Wow!' said Emmy, 'you must have been exhausted!'

Jon shook his head. 'I really enjoy what I do - and the thought that I was building up enough cash to get out of that damned bedsit didn't hurt either. Then, when I'd finished, Horace took me for Sunday lunch at the pub - and that was it - one taste of Lucy's roast and I was a goner!' he laughed.

'I can imagine,' Emmy smiled. 'But how did you end up living here?'

'By the time I'd driven down for my third roast in a row, I'd started getting to know the locals. I'd already started to ask around to see if there was anywhere available to rent. The pub was mega-busy, and Ali invited me to share her table. The rest, as they say, is history. Little Bamton is my home.'

Emmy nodded. 'Any luck finding somewhere else to rent yet?'

Jon shook his head. 'Nah. But I'm in no rush. As long as I'm out of here by the autumn, that's soon enough for me. I just really want to find somewhere here in the village.'

Emmy nodded again, privately thinking to herself that the feeling was entirely mutual.

'Thanks for telling me,' she said, turning and planting a kiss on his shoulder.

Jon smiled at her and planted a kiss on top of her head. Emmy practically melted.

Thump-thump-thump!

The knock on the caravan door made them both jump.

Jon hastily stood, pulled on a pair of jeans and went over to answer it. As soon as he opened the door, Charlie dashed in.

'Huh, the cat's learned to knock,' he chuckled, as he turned to watch Charlie leap lightly onto the bed.

Emmy reached out a hand and stroked his head, eliciting an instant, rumbling purr.

'Hey Jon, have you seen Emmy? All the lights are on over at the cottage, but she's not answering her phone or the door. I'm a bit worried.'

It was Caro's voice.

'Sure. She's right here,' answered Jon. 'I'll go help Sam unload and you two can catch up. Two secs.'

Jon walked back towards the bed, bent low and kissed Emmy, before snagging a tee shirt and sweater off the floor, dragging them on and heading out in his welly boots.

Emmy quickly pulled the duvet up to her chin as Caro stepped into the caravan.

'Well well well, Emmy Martin, you little hussy,' she grinned.

Emmy couldn't help but beam back at her friend.

By the time Emmy had explained to Caro *most* of what had happened the previous evening over a pilfered cup of coffee, Sam and Jon had finished unloading Sam's pick-up and had carted all the wood for the raised beds into the paddock.

'Thank you so much!' beamed Emmy. 'I'm Emmy by the way,' she said, holding her hand out to Sam who gave it a hearty shake.

'So I gathered,' he said with a grin. 'And it's no problem. I wasn't sure how many you were planning to make - this should be enough for two, but I can bring down as much as you need if you want to expand.'

Emmy smiled at him. 'Two is perfect to start with - though I went a bit mad on my dream-plans. I've got eight on there, as well as a massive three-bin compost system, a polytunnel and an area for shrubs,' she laughed.

'You do?!' said Jon.

Emmy nodded. 'I know I'm only here for a little while longer, but it was a kind-of dream-scenario-thing. I emailed a photo of it to Ali for her amusement. A lot of fun to think about, even if it'll never happen.'

Her smile faltered briefly at the thought of leaving, but she quickly batted it away. Today was about beginnings, not endings.

'So, would you guys like a hand to put the two beds together?' asked Sam. 'We're off out for a walk on the moors now, but we could come back and lend a hand this afternoon if you'd like?'

Emmy shook her head. 'That's really kind, but I wanted to have a chat with Alf first. Ali said he'd be able to help me make sure the beds were in the best spot.'

'Well then, you're in luck. I saw him yesterday and he said he was going to pay you a visit on his way down to Sunday lunch,' said Caro.

'He did?' asked Emmy. 'But I've never met him... how would he know...?'

'I'd hazard a guess that it isn't just you that Ali's been emailing,' laughed Jon. 'In fact...' he held up a finger.

'What?' said Emmy.

'Listen! he said.

SPRING FLOWERS AND APRIL SHOWERS

She strained her ears and caught the sound of hooves clopping up the lane in their direction.

Emmy peered over towards the gate which was still standing open from where the boys had been bringing the wood in. A gorgeous, stocky silver horse appeared and plodded into the paddock, led by an elderly man in a flat-cap. On the other side of the horse walked a man who looked like he'd taken a wrong turning. He was wearing a dark grey suit, complete with waistcoat and shiny black brogues.

'Alf!' cried Sam, greeting the gent in the flat cap as they drew near.

'Hello Thor, my beautiful boy!' crooned Caro, hurrying to take the lead-rope from Alf and throw her arms around the horse's neck.

Emmy couldn't help but smile at the sight of the little horse closing his eyes and leaning his head heavily over her friend's shoulder.

'Don't mind those two,' laughed Alf, 'that was love at first sight! Nice to meet you, Emmy!' he said, holding out his hand.

Emmy grinned at him and shook it gladly. 'Thanks so much for coming over - I didn't know-'

'Your aunt said you could do with a bit of growing advice in her last message, so I thought I'd nip over and see what was what. But before we get into all that, I picked this gent up down by the bridges. Mr Hall? This is Emmy - she's stayin' at Dragonfly, and that there's Jon Clark.'

The mysterious Mr Hall stepped forward. 'Jon, I think you're expecting me?'

Emmy glanced at him, but Jon looked dumbfounded.

'Ali and I had an appointment today,' said Mr Hall, looking concerned, 'but that was set up before she made her plans for Australia. She said that she'd asked you to deal with it for her instead?'

'Appointment?' said Jon, still looking confused.

'Yes - to do a valuation of Dragonfly Cottage.'

CHAPTER 19

'Wait, what?' said Emmy faintly, trying to catch up.

'A valuation of the cottage,' repeated Mr Hall.

'On a Sunday?' said Emmy.

Mr Hall nodded, and Sam discreetly wandered over towards Caro, Alf and Thor, giving the three of them a little privacy.

'Ali and I are old friends, though I've never been to visit her out here. So, our plan was for me to do the inspection required for the report, and then we were going to go to the pub for Sunday lunch together. I didn't see there was any need to cancel when Ali decided to book her trip.'

'Of course,' said Jon, recognition dawning on his face. 'Mr Hall, I'm so sorry, I have to admit that it had completely slipped my mind.'

'You *knew?!*' squeaked Emmy.

Jon nodded. 'Ali mentioned it to me ages ago, before we knew you'd be coming to stay in the cottage.'

'Oh.'

'Would you prefer to show Mr Hall-'

'Please, call me Arthur, dear boy!'

Jon nodded. 'Emmy, would you prefer to show Arthur around?'

Emmy shook her head quickly. 'I need to talk to Alf,' she said shortly.

Jon shot her a concerned look.

'If you don't mind doing it?' she checked quickly.

'Of course not. Arthur, if you'd like to come with me?'

'You know,' he said, turning to follow Jon towards the paddock gate, 'this field could be worth a pretty penny if she could get planning for some development on it.'

Emmy's heart dropped into her boots. What was happening? This had started out as the perfect day and now it was disintegrating into some kind of nightmare.

Sam and Caro quickly said their goodbyes and headed off for their walk, but Emmy caught their concerned glances as they closed the gate on their way out of the paddock.

'Now then, lass. Don't you go worrying about things that are outside your control,' said Alf kindly. He unclipped Thor's lead rope and the little horse instantly dropped his head and started ripping up gobfuls of lush, spring grass.

'But… she's selling?' said Emmy, feeling completely dazed.

'I don't know I'm afraid. Let's focus on what we do know. You want two beds for growing cut flowers - that right?'

Emmy nodded, desperately trying to bring her attention back to Alf and the job in hand. But as he talked about making sure that the beds weren't too wide, and pointing out things like natural wind protection and the way the sun travelled across the paddock, her heart just wasn't in it.

Why put in all this work when she would have to leave Dragonfly Cottage before the flowers would even be out. It had been different when she'd been expecting to move out in time to welcome her aunt home, but to see strangers move in and sweep away all her precious memories? There just wasn't any point.

~

'Why didn't you tell me Aunty Ali was planning to sell Dragonfly?' demanded Emmy as soon as Jon came within earshot of her perch on the caravan's steps.

Alf had left about twenty minutes ago, promising as much well-rotted manure as her heart desired, as well as some of his own precious seedlings. But she'd barely managed to thank him. She was pretty sure her heart was breaking.

'Woah, Emmy!' said Jon, his hands up in front of

him, a pained look on his face. 'Firstly - I'm really sorry I didn't tell you about the appointment, but Ali mentioned it in passing ages ago and I'd completely forgotten about it.'

'Is he over there now?' she demanded, a wobble in her voice.

Jon shook his head, frowning in concern. 'No, he's gone over to the pub for lunch. He's got all the info he needs. Anyway, what makes you think Ali's planning to sell?'

Emmy rolled her eyes. 'Duh, why else would she get the place valued?!'

'Any number of reasons,' said Jon, sounding a bit frustrated now. 'Insurance. Remortgaging. Maybe even making a will?'

Emmy huffed and shook her head.

'Emmy,' sighed Jon, reaching out, taking her hands and pulling her to her feet, 'look, I really don't know why Ali decided to get the place valued, but believe me, if I did know, I would have told you. You do believe me, don't you?'

Emmy sighed and her whole body seemed to sag. She nodded and smiled weakly at Jon. 'Sorry,' she said. 'I'm just a bit wiped.'

Jon wrapped his arms around her. She hugged him back briefly but then pulled away. Everything felt wrong somehow. 'I'm going to head back to the cottage for a bit if that's okay?'

'Oh, sure!' he said. 'Then we'll meet back up later to

get the beds in place? I'm guessing Alf has suggested the best place for them?'

She nodded. 'Yeah, he did. But... if it's okay with you, I'd like to look over my plans again. Maybe we can do it one evening, or maybe next weekend?'

'Sure. Whatever you want,' he said, thrusting his hands into his pockets and giving her a smile that didn't quite reach his eyes.

Emmy felt another little crack appear in her heart as she turned and headed back towards the cottage alone.

∽

Emmy had spent the whole afternoon searching for nearby jobs on the internet. If her aunt was going to sell Dragonfly Cottage, she wouldn't have access to the gardens or the paddock either. It meant that her dream would come to an end at the same time as her three months in the cottage. It was time to stop deluding herself that she was going to somehow make this work. She needed to start looking for a job and, very soon, she'd need to start looking for a new home too.

It was supper time when her grumbling stomach finally forced her to surface. She'd reached the dreg-ends of the listings anyway. The jobs had descended to those that were so vaguely worded they could involve anything from lama-smuggling to topless-dancing.

There was no work in floristry anywhere nearby,

nor anything even remotely related to it. Just a couple of weeks ago, this wouldn't have bothered her so much - she'd have been happy to take a bit of temp work to bring some cash in. But Little Bamton had changed her. She was no longer willing to compromise on the things that brought joy into her life. Which left her with only one choice. She'd have to find a job that suited her, and go wherever it took her.

The thought of leaving Little Bamton, leaving her new friends - leaving Jon - caused the tears to well in her eyes and trickle, unchecked, down her cheeks.

Emmy jumped as Charlie landed in his not-so-light-footed fashion next to her on the sofa and meowed.

'I know, I know - it's your teatime,' she said, reaching out to stroke his head. 'Mine too - come on, let's see what we can find.'

She barely tasted the slices of cheese on toast, but she forced them down just for something to do. Jon had texted her several times during the day, checking that she was alright. She'd replied, pleading tiredness, but as yet another one popped up asking if she'd like some company, she realised that she'd better make her excuses for the night. There was no way she was fit to see anyone right now.

She quickly sent him one back saying that she was going to turn in early, as soon as she'd picked and prepped her flowers, and that she'd see him in the morning.

Huh. Flowers. For the first time since she'd started the stall, Emmy wasn't looking forward to going out into the garden to choose the blooms. Every single stem would just be a reminder that the lovely garden where all her childhood memories were stored would soon belong to someone else.

No. There was no way she could face it. Little Bamton would simply have to do without her stall tomorrow. She was going to bed.

～

Emmy woke the next morning feeling like she'd swallowed a lead weight. Despite going to bed early, she'd slept badly, plagued by the old *Daisy Days* nightmares again. Dragging herself out of bed, she pulled on a tatty pair of jeans and an old sweater that used to belong to Grandad Jim.

She needed coffee. She grabbed her phone to check the time. Half nine. Huh. Well, there was definitely no chance of getting the flower stall done now, even if she'd wanted to. Which she didn't.

There were three texts from Jon, and one missed call. She swiped through and read them all, and then sighed. Poor Jon, they'd had such an amazing time together, and then she'd just lost it. And now he was worried about her because he'd noticed that the flowers weren't out. The last text said that he would be letting himself into the cottage to check that she was okay if he hadn't heard from her by ten.

Okay, new plan. Text Jon, then coffee. The last thing she needed was for him to come on some kind of rescue mission. She knew she owed him a proper apology, she just needed to be sufficiently caffeinated to do it.

Hey. I'm okay - just slept late. Will pop over and see you this afternoon. Em x

She trundled down the stairs and only just managed to avoid tripping over a decidedly disgruntled Charlie, who yowled at her in disgust.

'Alright, alright, new plan,' sighed Emmy. 'Feed Charlie, then make coffee.'

She'd just placed a dish of jelly down in front of the ravenous cat when her phone started to ring.

'Nooo, I need coffee!' she yelled at it, before flipping the case open and spotting an international number.

She quickly accepted the call. 'Hello?'

'Emmy? It's Aunty Ali.'

'Hi!' she said, smiling in spite of herself.

'Jon says you're sulking.'

'He... what?!' spluttered Emmy.

'He was really worried about you when you didn't put your flowers out this morning. He seems to think you've got some ridiculous notion about me selling Dragonfly?'

'Wait - he *told* on me?!' squeaked Emmy, sounding like a six-year-old.

SPRING FLOWERS AND APRIL SHOWERS

'Well, was he right?'

'Maybe,' mumbled Emmy.

'Oh, Em!' sighed her aunt.

'Wait, what time is it there?' asked Emmy.

'Just before eight in the evening - now, stop trying to wriggle out of talking to me!' she laughed. 'You always were a one for that, ever since you were little.'

Emmy rolled her eyes. There was something so comforting, yet so very annoying, about talking to someone who almost knew you better than you knew yourself.

'Tell me what's wrong,' said her aunt gently.

'Mr Hall came to value the cottage.'

'I asked Arthur to. He's a good friend.'

'But why? Are you selling?'

'No… at least, not quite yet.'

'What?!'

'Emmy, you've got to understand. I love the village. I love Dragonfly - it's been my home nearly all my life. For you, it's filled with memories of a lovely childhood and a doting family. But for me - I've also got memories of losing both my mum and my dad there. And that's really hard to live with.'

Emmy swallowed. 'I'm sorry - I never thought about that.'

'And I wouldn't want you to!' she said, decidedly. 'I didn't mean it like that, Em. But being away has made me feel lighter, happier, like I can get away from the darker memories and my grief for a while. And knowing that you're there, enjoying the place - that's even better.'

'But you might sell it?' asked Emmy.

'Maybe one day.'

'Oh.'

'Em - you've got to remember that you haven't even been to visit since Grandad Jim died. I don't blame you, really I don't - I know first-hand how hard it is to be there without him. And I know how much you were struggling with your own problems - with work and that awful ex of yours.'

'Yeah, well...'

'I'm not having a go - just explaining why I was gathering my options.'

'I wish I could buy it from you,' Emmy blurted. She'd never even dared admit that thought to herself before, let alone say it out loud.

'You really mean that?' asked Ali steadily.

Emmy nodded. 'I do. But there's no chance of that at the moment. But if I can't live here at Dragonfly, I've decided that I want to stay in Little Bamton if I can. I still want to grow and sell my flowers. It's what I love - so I need to find a way, somehow.'

'Then I've got an idea. Emmy - I really want to carry on travelling. My visa here runs out at the end of the three months, but I'd love to visit your mum in Portugal for a while, and I've always wanted to explore Scandinavia.'

'Wow! So...'

'So, how would you fancy renting Dragonfly from me - for a year to begin with? I'd give you reduced rent in return for keeping my stuff there as it is.'

'You mean it?'

'What do you think?'

'Oh, Aunty Ali - I'd love to!'

'And what about Charlie?'

'We're best friends,' she laughed. 'It wouldn't be the same here without him.'

'Yay! That's wonderful news! Okay - it's a deal. I'll email you with some details by the end of the week and we can go from there.'

'Thank you so much!' breathed Emmy, barely able to believe that this was happening.

'I just want you to be happy. We're all so proud of you, Em, and I know your Grandad Jim would be too.'

Emmy couldn't do anything more than snivel down the phone for a moment.

'Now that we've got all that sorted, would you please go and put that poor boy out of his misery?' she demanded.

Emmy laughed. 'Me and Jon-'

'Yes, I thought you two might hit it off,' laughed Ali. 'He's a lovely lad.'

'He is.'

'And just to say - if you ever fancied a house-mate, well - I'd be happy to give him a good character reference!'

Emmy grinned. She knew exactly what her aunt was getting at.

'Now then, my girl - get ready, you've got a big day ahead of you. And it's all going to start with a knock on the door in exactly sixty seconds. Love you!'

Emmy stared in confusion at her phone. Had they been cut off? No - it looked like her aunt had just hung up. What on earth?

There was a loud knock at the front door.

CHAPTER 20

'Violet?!'

Emmy threw the door open wider and gawped.

'No need for the goldfish impression dear,' said Violet with a wry smile.

Emmy quickly closed her mouth.

'May I come in?'

'Of course,' said Emmy, quickly standing aside to let the upright old lady pass her in the hall. She turned and slowly shut the door.

Aunty Ali, what are you up to?

'Do hurry, dear, we don't have all day,' Violet's voice drifted through from the kitchen.

Emmy hurried along the hall to find that Violet had already parked herself at the table and laid a document case in front of her.

'To what do I owe the pleasure…?'

'We have things to discuss, Emmy.'

'O-kay... would you like a cup of tea?'

Violet pulled back the cuff of her cashmere cardigan and glanced at a little gold watch on her wrist before answering. 'Yes. That's a good idea.'

Emmy nodded, filled the kettle and flicked it on. A buzzing sound made her turn, only to find Violet checking the screen of a rather snazzy iPhone.

'Now then, I understand congratulations are in order. Welcome - more permanently - to Little Bamton!' she said with a smile.

'Thank you,' said Emmy, surprised, 'but how-?'

'The miracles of modern technology, dear,' said Violet, waggling the mobile at her before slipping it back in her pocket. 'Now then. I don't know if you are aware that I was very good friends with your grandparents?'

Emmy placed a mug of tea in front of Violet, followed by a little jug of milk and the sugar bowl before shaking her head.

'No, I didn't,' she said.

Violet nodded with a sad smile. 'I miss them both terribly.' She paused and cleared her throat. 'When your grandmother passed away, Jim made some necessary alterations to their will. I am one of the executors.'

'Oh, right,' said Emmy. She didn't have a clue where this was going, but a sudden wave of nerves washed over her.

'As you know, he left this cottage to your mother

and aunt. Ali then bought your mother out after six months.'

Emmy nodded. She remembered because it had given her mum the cash to relocate permanently to Portugal.

'Jim also left something to you.'

Emmy nodded again. 'A thousand pounds,' she said quietly.

'Yes. But he also left you something else,' said Violet carefully.

'No, just the money, and mum and Aunty Ali let me choose a few of his things too.'

'There is something else, but it came with certain conditions that mean you've only just become eligible to receive it.'

'What?' said Emmy in surprise, 'I don't understand.'

'Jim loved you very much, Emmy.'

Emmy nodded, a lump forming in her throat.

'It's probably best that it comes from him,' said Violet gently. She unzipped the case in front of her, drew out an envelope and handed it to Emmy.

She took it with shaking fingers, looking down at her name, printed across the front in Grandad Jim's slightly shaky handwriting, familiar from so many white seed labels she'd seen him fill out over the years.

She opened the envelope and pulled out the folded piece of paper inside.

. . .

My darling Emmy-Lou,

If you're reading this, then I'm afraid we won't have seen each other for quite a while. But you've chosen to try your hand at the life I've always dreamed of for you - a life filled with flowers.

Let me explain. I am leaving Dragonfly's paddock to you - but there are conditions - which I'll set out below. If these are not met, the paddock will remain attached to Dragonfly Cottage and in the care of your mother and aunt. No need to worry - the fact that you've got this letter in your hands means that you've already met most of them!

1. You are no longer in a relationship with that Chris boy. I'm sorry Emmy, but I don't trust him and I don't think he is good for you. If you're reading this, then congratulations on getting rid of him. I hope he didn't hurt you, and I hope that being back here in Little Bamton is helping you to remember who you really are.

2. You must come back and call Little Bamton your home for more than just a few days.

3. You must be working with - or wishing to work with - plants and flowers. Make the paddock a part of your plans, Emmy. I have a feeling that it will give you everything you need.

4. Now, this is the condition for the future. The land must not be sold for development. If you choose to look into building a potting shed or two, or even your own home one day so that you can be closer to the flowers that you love so much, then that's different. I trust you to do it in a way that is gentle and good for the whole village.

I leave it up to your mother, aunt and my dear friend Violet to judge when it is time for you to take ownership. Things are difficult for you right now, but I know you'll find your way home.

All that's left for me to do is tell you that I am so very proud of you. You have been one of the brightest lights in my life. I love you, Emmy-Lou, and I'll be there with you in every flower that you grow.

All my love, until we meet again,
Grandad Jim
xxx

Emmy felt two giant tears roll down her cheeks and watched as they plopped onto the table in front of her. She hastily wiped them away and looked up only to find that Violet was fiddling with her iPhone again, giving her the chance to get command of herself before trying to speak.

She cleared her throat, hoping it would help dislodge the lump of emotion that had lodged in her chest.

'Well, Emmy,' said Violet, looking up at her with a soft smile.

'I can't believe it,' she whispered. 'It's like Grandad Jim's reaching out to make my dreams come true.'

Violet gently shook her head. 'As much as your Grandad doted upon you my dear, it's your own actions that have made this happen.'

Emmy stood up and grabbed a piece of kitchen roll from the counter to wipe her eyes and blow her nose.

'All the official paperwork is with Jim's solicitor of course, and I can give you all the details you need so that the papers are transferred to your name.'

Emmy nodded, barely able to believe this was happening.

'I trust,' said Violet in a sterner tone of voice, 'that this means I won't have to go without my daily bunch of flowers again?'

Emmy shot her a wobbly smile and nodded.

'Good. Now then, young lady, we have somewhere we need to be in five minutes. I suggest you go and wash your face - and maybe change, too?'

∼

It took Emmy quite a lot longer than five minutes to pull herself together and make herself look presentable. She had absolutely no idea where Violet was about to take her, but she definitely didn't want to step out of the house looking like Charlie had mauled her in the night.

Speaking of the cat, when she re-entered the kitchen - complete with freshly brushed hair, a slightly less crumpled jumper, and even a sweep of mascara - Charlie was happily ensconced on Violet's lap, totally blissed-out as she tickled him behind the ears.

'This lump needs to go on a diet!' tutted Violet as she gently lifted him down.

Emmy smirked.

'Ready?' asked Violet, picking up her folder.

'Erm... where are we going?'

'It's a surprise.'

'Oh. Okay.'

Emmy followed Violet to the door, thinking that no surprise could top the two she'd already received that morning. She laboured under this comfortable delusion until she found herself standing at the paddock gate. Hanging from the front of it was a beautifully painted banner that declared they'd reached *Grandad Jim's Flower Farm.*

Emmy gasped, recognising Eve's gorgeous handiwork. She only tore her eyes away from it when she heard the cheering drifting across the paddock.

'Come along, Emmy, don't keep your friends waiting!' said Violet, grabbing her hand and towing her briskly into the field.

Emmy instantly regretted the mascara. There, cheering and clapping, were Sue and Lucy, Caro and Sam, Amber, Eve and Alf. Even Thor was there, though he was far too busy munching away at the grass to notice her arrival.

Right at the middle of them all was Jon, a huge grin on his face as he whooped and clapped. Then he pointed and she tore her gaze away from him to look.

Emmy froze. *No way!*

There, in the exact spot she and Alf had decided upon yesterday were eight newly-built raised beds. They were set out exactly as she'd drawn them in her plan. Her *dream*-plan.

'How-?!'

She turned to look at Violet and the old woman tutted again. 'I keep telling you dear, modern technology!'

Emmy turned back to the beds again, unable to believe they were real.

'Ali emailed me the picture of the plan you sent her,' said Alf, a massive smile on his face as he strode up to her. 'All they need now is mulching and filling and you'll be well away! Did we get them right?'

'They're... they're perfect!' said Emmy, then promptly burst into tears.

Jon hurried over to her and wrapped his arms around her.

'Hey! You okay?' he asked, surprise and concern in his voice.

'I'm... just... so... happy!' she wailed, burying her head in his chest.

It took her several moments to calm down enough to hug everyone else in turn.

'I don't know what to say,' she said when she'd been around twice, finally stopping when Jon wrapped an arm tightly around her shoulders. 'Thank you all so much. I'm guessing Ali told you all that I'm the new owner of the paddock?' she asked, trying to take it all in.

Amber nodded at her from across the little circle, grinning.

'And the other bit of news is that I'm going to be staying in Little Bamton.'

Jon swung her around to face him.

'You mean it?!' he demanded. In that moment, he looked so hopeful, so vulnerable that Emmy wanted to ask him to move in with her on the spot. But no, they had plenty of time to get there now. Thanks to her aunt, they had all the time in the world.

'I mean it,' she said, 'I've got the cottage for at least another year.'

Before she could say another word, Jon gathered her up and kissed her.

By the time they broke apart, Emmy was breathless, but she couldn't help grinning at the whoops and the cheers coming from the others.

'Oi you two, we haven't finished yet - and I've got a pub to open!' laughed Lucy.

'How can there be more?!' gasped Emmy. 'This has already been the best day I've ever had.'

'It's not over yet, love!' said Sue, beaming at her.

Amber and Caro strode towards her, grabbed a hand each and towed her towards Jon's caravan.

'What the-'

'Well, we had to hide it somewhere!' giggled Eve as she strode along with them.

They lead her into his little garden where there was a massive - *something* - hidden under a large, white bed-sheet.

'Sam - I think you'd better do the honours!' commanded Jon, as they all piled into the little space, Violet bringing up the rear, leaning on Alf's arm.

Sam stepped forward and grabbed a corner of the sheet.

'Three... two... one!' he yelled.

The sheet fell to the floor and Emmy couldn't help the shriek that escaped her, much to the amusement of everyone else.

It was a massive, wooden flower cart. With two wheels at one end and gorgeously carved wooden handles at the other, it was a thing of absolute beauty. There were three levels of shelves and a wide, flat base, all nestling under a cleverly designed roof that would keep the weather off her precious flowers.

Hanging from a couple of chains was a curved, hand-carved sign. *Grandad Jim's Flowers.*

Emmy stepped forward and ran her fingers over the letters, fighting the tears that were determined to escape again.

'What do you think?' asked Sam. 'Look there's even a built-in money-box here with a little lock! You don't have to use it, but we thought you might like-'

'You made this? For me?' Emmy blubbed, turning to him.

Sam nodded.

'I love it. I can't believe... thank you! Thank you so much. I don't know how to-'

'Don't miss the fliers Eve made for you!' said Amber, pointing at a little stack of papers that had been weighted down with a stone.

Emmy picked one up with shaking fingers. There was her little flower cart, turned into the perfect logo, along with her mobile number and email address.

She couldn't get the words out and simply turned and hugged Eve tightly.

'Right you lovely lot,' laughed Lucy, 'how about we all head to the pub?'

Jon nodded, taking hold of Emmy's hand and giving it a squeeze.

'Oh, and Emmy? I reckon it's book club at your place next,' grinned Sue. 'That means you get to choose the book.'

'I'd love that! How about...' Emmy glanced up at Jon then back at the others, 'Lady Chatterley's Lover?'

Jon spluttered, sending the rest of them into a fit of giggles.

The pair of them hung back a moment as the others started making their way towards the paddock gate. Emmy went to gaze at her cart again and Jon came to stand behind her, wrapping his arms tightly around her.

'You okay?' he asked gently, kissing the top of her head.

'I can't believe this is all happening!' she sighed,

leaning back into him. 'Living at Dragonfly, owning this field. You. Us. It's like a dream. It's... just...'

'Perfect.' Jon finished for her.

Emmy turned to face him. 'Perfect,' she echoed, reaching up to kiss him. In that moment, she knew she was exactly where she was meant to be.

Home.

THE END

ALSO BY BETH RAIN

Little Bamton Series:

Little Bamton: The Complete Series Collection: Books 1 - 5

Individual titles:

Christmas Lights and Snowball Fights (Little Bamton Book 1)

Spring Flowers and April Showers (Little Bamton Book 2)

Summer Nights and Pillow Fights (Little Bamton Book 3)

Autumn Cuddles and Muddy Puddles (Little Bamton Book 4)

Christmas Flings and Wedding Rings (Little Bamton Book 5)

Upper Bamton Series:

A New Arrival in Upper Bamton (Upper Bamton Book 1)

Rainy Days in Upper Bamton (Upper Bamton Book 2)

Hidden Treasures in Upper Bamton (Upper Bamton Book 3)

Time Flies By in Upper Bamton (Upper Bamton Book 4)

Seabury Series:

Welcome to Seabury (Seabury Book 1)

Trouble in Seabury (Seabury Book 2)

Christmas in Seabury (Seabury Book 3)

Sandwiches in Seabury (Seabury Book 4)

Secrets in Seabury (Seabury Book 5)

Surprises in Seabury (Seabury Book 6)

Dreams and Ice Creams in Seabury (Seabury Book 7)

Mistakes and Heartbreaks in Seabury (Seabury Book 8)

Laughter and Happy Ever After in Seabury (Seabury Book 9)

Seabury Series Collections:

Kate's Story: Books 1 - 3

Hattie's Story: Books 4 - 6

Writing as Bea Fox:

What's a Girl To Do? The Complete Series

Individual titles:

The Holiday: What's a Girl To Do? (Book 1)

The Wedding: What's a Girl To Do? (Book 2)

The Lookalike: What's a Girl To Do? (Book 3)

The Reunion: What's a Girl To Do? (Book 4)

At Christmas: What's a Girl To Do? (Book 5)

ABOUT THE AUTHOR

Beth Rain has always wanted to be a writer and has been penning adventures for characters ever since she learned to stare into the middle-distance and daydream.

She currently lives in the (sometimes) sunny South West, and it is a dream come true to spend her days hanging out with Bob – her trusty laptop – scoffing crisps and chocolate while dreaming up swoony love stories for all her imaginary friends.

Beth's writing will always deliver on the happy-ever-afters, so if you need cosy… you're in safe hands!

Visit www.bethrain.com for all the bookish goodness and keep up with all Beth's news by joining her monthly newsletter!

facebook.com/BethRainBooks
twitter.com/bethrainauthor
instagram.com/bethrainauthor